CUT THE LIGHTS

Karen Krossing

ORCA BOOK PUBLISHERS

Library and Archives Canada Cataloguing in Publication

Krossing, Karen, 1965-
Cut the lights / Karen Krossing.
(Orca limelights)

Issued also in electronic format.
ISBN 978-1-4598-0413-5

I. Title. II. Series: Orca limelights
PS8571.R776C87 2013   jc813'.6   C2013-901911-1

First published in the United States, 2013
Library of Congress Control Number: 2013935386

Summary: Briar has been chosen to direct a one-act play at her
performing arts high school, but she learns there's more to it than imposing
her vision on the cast and crew.

MIX
Paper from
responsible sources
FSC   FSC® C016245
www.fsc.org

*Orca Book Publishers is dedicated to preserving the environment and has
printed this book on Forest Stewardship Council® certified paper.*

Orca Book Publishers gratefully acknowledges the support for
its publishing programs provided by the following agencies:
the Government of Canada through the Canada Book Fund and the
Canada Council for the Arts, and the Province of British Columbia
through the BC Arts Council and the Book Publishing Tax Credit.

Design by Teresa Bubela
Cover photography by Getty Images

ORCA BOOK PUBLISHERS
PO Box 5626, STN. B
Victoria, BC Canada
V8R 6S4

ORCA BOOK PUBLISHERS
PO Box 468
Custer, WA USA
98240-0468

www.orcabook.com
Printed and bound in Canada.

16 15 14 13 • 4 3 2 1

For Paige and Tess, who shared their stories.

One

A tidy kitchen. Early morning. A vase of lilies sits on the granite countertop.

My parents chew their oatmeal without talking. Dad stares steadily out the window at the lilac blooms. Mom reads the newspaper folded beside her bowl. Upstairs, Mom's much younger sister, Darla, thumps from room to room, hollering about a lost nose ring, threatening to bring her chaos downstairs.

I slip on my new glasses—red cat's-eye frames, no lenses—and position myself near the sink so I can see the table and hall.

"Glasses?" My mother looks puzzled. "But your eyes are fine, Briar."

"Yup. They have no frames, so I can see clearly." I poke my fingers out through the eyeholes and wiggle them around. "It's symbolic."

"Why are you wearing them?" Her nose wrinkles.

"Is this a trend at that school of yours?" Dad lowers his spoon.

"Trends are for followers," I explain, even though it's pointless. "These glasses remind me to think like a theater director—they frame the scene."

Mom pinches her lips together.

"You're still talking about directing?" Dad's tone of voice says he hopes I'll outgrow it.

"Yup." I pour myself a glass of mango juice, imagining a rosy future where my parents accept my dreams as more than whimsy. Impossible, I know, but before you judge them, try to understand. Dad is a bookkeeper. Not a useless profession; even theater directors need to track budgets and maybe even ticket sales. Mom's job is more baffling—she's an office manager at a sock company. The place is painfully practical—unless you make sock puppets and put on a show. I got in trouble for doing that on "Take Your Kid to Work" day.

"Where would you get a job as a director?" Dad asks.

I'm ready with numbers—it helps to speak his language. "Did you know that last year there were 227 productions in this city?" I down my juice and pocket a granola bar for later.

"Really." Dad frowns.

"That includes 187 professional companies with 62 venues and over 38,000 seats, not including outdoor venues, theaters with less than 400 seats or comedy clubs."

"You seem to know what you're talking about." Dad raises his eyebrows.

"Yup." I smile, just as my aunt Darla clomps down the stairs in her high-heeled boots. I adjust my glasses, ready to view the full impact of the upcoming drama.

"Morning." Darla twists her nose ring into place.

Dad grimaces and Mom nods. I wave hello, admiring how the sunlight cuts between Darla and my parents, dividing the kitchen in two. As Darla turns to the coffeemaker, her oversized fair-trade bag from Nepal knocks over the vase on the island.

"Darla!" Mom leaps to catch the vase. She ends up with her blouse drenched and lilies spilling down her front, but she catches the vase before it shatters.

Darla swings around, wide-eyed. "Did I do that?"

If this were a stage, I'd put a mic over the island to capture the dialogue.

Dad sighs and rubs his eyes.

Mom grabs a clean dishtowel and starts mopping up water, her forehead creased.

"Let me help." Darla plucks lilies off the floor, setting them in the vase at bizarre angles. "I've got a job interview with Finders Keepers this morning—they find odd props for TV commercials. Maybe this time I'll get lucky!" Darla calls herself an actress, although she hardly ever gets called for auditions anymore. Now she's trying to get a behind-the-scenes job.

"Maybe this time you'll keep a job for more than two weeks," Dad mutters. He hates it when Darla is out of work because she always moves in with us. She's been here two months this time— long enough to set him on edge.

Mom rearranges the jumbled flowers while giving Darla a disapproving look. "Why can't you get an ordinary job like everyone else?"

I consider reblocking the scene—turning Darla's body toward the audience, and moving Dad so Mom's not masking him.

"Why would I want to do that?" Darla plants her hands on her hips.

I leave for school, promising myself I'll be anything but ordinary.

* * *

A school hallway buzzes with students. Ten minutes to first class.

Sonata, the best actor in the school, waltzes past in a white minidress with strategic rips in all the right places. A guy dressed like Alfred Hitchcock films a kid with a purple mohawk. Two grade-twelve girls sing *Phantom of the Opera* songs at full volume. Like Principal Racier says at every assembly, "You can be anything you want at Whitlock School of the Arts."

Ratna waits by my locker, fidgeting. She's petite, fine-boned, a brilliant playwright and my best friend.

"Nice glasses." She tucks her black, bobbed hair behind her ears.

"Thanks. They're my director frames."

Ratna shoots me a sideways look, but it's brief. My glasses may seem radical compared to my plain jeans and *Stage Crew* T-shirt, but I'm not that weird for Whitlock. Last year, I joined the stage crew so I'd know enough about lighting and sound to direct a play this year.

"I'm hoping my glasses bring me good luck today." I cross my fingers and toes. "Is the list up?" Mr. Ty, the lead drama teacher, promised to post the list of student-written plays and student directors selected for this year's Whitlock Fringe Festival "at first light on April third"—his exact words.

"Not yet." Ratna chews a fingernail. "But we should look again."

"Definitely."

As we link arms and march toward the drama office, I swallow hard. *Wish Upon a Star*, written by Ratna and to be directed by me, just has to be listed. It would be my directorial debut, apart from short skits in drama classes. It's only a one-act play, but I know I can still create a masterpiece of sound, lights, set and performance.

"I want to cast Sonata for the lead," I say, to distract myself from the idea that we might not get listed.

"Every director will want her, Briar. You'll never get her."

"I will when she reads the lines you wrote." I elbow her.

Ratna smiles at the compliment. "But she always works with Lorna."

"Hey, seniors aren't the only talent in this school," I say, even though Lorna's an awesome director.

"I know." Ratna shrugs.

We walk in silence.

"If we don't get picked, will you audition?" she asks.

"Never." I make a face. "I hate acting." I don't mention that acting makes me nervous.

"But you take drama!"

"Only because I want to direct. Directing has more..." I pause to find the right words. "Artistic control. With *Wish Upon a Star*, I was thinking—"

I break off as we round the corner and see a crowd gathered outside Mr. Ty's office.

"The list!" Ratna grabs my hand.

"Only seven plays selected."

"More than thirty submitted."

I frown. "Let's get it over with."

As we get closer, my stomach lurches and my canvas Toms shoes feel like lead. I wish everyone would vanish—I won't be able to bear the humiliation if Ratna and I aren't listed.

We elbow into the crowd. Sonata is there already, congratulating Lorna. Apparently, she'll be directing a play she also wrote. Impressive. I can see over the heads to the sheet taped to Mr. Ty's door. Before we get near, Lorna claps both Ratna and me on the back. "Way to go, you two!"

My mouth goes dry. "We made it?"

Ratna looks stunned, and then a grin widens her tiny face.

"You're the only grade tens on the list." Lorna smirks like she has a secret. "So if you need any directing tips, Briar, I can..."

"I'm fine," I say quickly. I don't need anyone's help.

Lorna looks down her long nose. "Of course you are." She turns away.

"We did it!" Ratna squeals before she disappears to read the list.

I watch her laugh with the others. Lorna hugs Sonata.

I straighten my glasses. Ratna's work is done. Mine is only beginning.

Two

The next day after classes. A drama room in the basement of Whitlock. Dark curtains. A purple carpet. Looming black wooden boxes of various sizes to use for staging. Spotlights heat up the low stage.

Mr. Ty stands in the hall, sending in actors one by one. I'm beside Lorna at the end of a row of seven directors fidgeting in chairs while watching auditions. We're all on edge, hoping to land the perfect cast. The room smells stale. The auditions feel stale too.

Each director takes a turn asking an actor to cold-read a page from his or her script. One actor blocked his face with the script while reading. Another droned in a flat, emotionless voice.

A grade-nine girl came in a fairy costume with sparkly wings—totally unprofessional, especially when she was asked to read the part of a ship's captain. Now we're listening to a senior girl give a long speech about why she's an amazing actor. I hike my glasses higher and picture her dressed in funeral black at her own hanging.

"Thanks for auditioning," I interrupt, even though she hasn't read one line from the script. I'm starting to wonder how I'll ever get a decent cast.

The girl stops abruptly, her hand flying to her throat. "But I didn't—"

"You'll be informed of any callbacks," Lorna adds. "The final list will be posted in a few days."

The girl flounces out of the room, her hair swinging.

"You can call her back, Lorna," says Samuel, a long-haired director who always wears plaid shirts with jeans. "She's all yours." He smirks.

"But you two would be perfect together." Lorna's smile is fake-sweet. "I insist you take her."

I shift uneasily, picturing lightning bolts sparking between Lorna and Samuel. Any director is a bit of a control freak, but seven in one room competing for actors is asking for trouble.

Luckily, Mr. Ty sends in the next actor pronto. It's a grade-eleven guy named Mica. He's pudgy and pale, with a face that shows how nervous he feels.

I perk up. Physically, he'd be a great male lead for my play if Sonata were my female lead. She's leggy and graceful—taller and thinner than him—and the contrast would be perfect. I have three parts to cast: a clueless husband, his demanding wife and the star she wishes on.

Mica heads to center stage. Ratna creeps up behind me—she must have snuck in with Mica.

"How's it going?" she whispers.

I lean back in my chair. "Better now. Mica could play opposite Sonata."

"You think he's a good choice?" Ratna eyes Mica doubtfully.

Lorna glares at me. "Sonata in your play? Dream on, Briar."

I ignore them both and give Mica my full attention. It's my turn to direct the audition, and he'll be reading from Ratna's script.

"Hi, Mica." I keep my tone friendly to put him at ease. "You'll be reading from *Wish Upon a Star* by Ratna Kapur." Behind me, Ratna makes a happy, squeaking noise in her throat.

"Not a very original title, Ratna," I hear Lorna whisper. "You may want to rethink."

"It's about a young wife who wishes upon a star to make improvements to her workaholic husband. It's very funny," I say a little too forcefully, glancing sideways at Lorna, daring her to contradict me. "You'll be reading the husband's monologue about his wife, Sylvia. The setting is a nineteen-fifties kitchen at night. Your wife is asleep in the next room, and you want a midnight snack." I pause, deciding to see what he can do on his own before directing him further. "Any time you're ready." I keep my expression neutral, even though I'm jittery too.

Mica takes a minute to read the script over and then begins.

"'I'm sure Sylvia didn't mean to burn the steak.'" He rubs his stomach as if he's hungry. "'She had a hard night. Really.'" He pleads for us to understand. "'Her car broke down. The dog threw up on her new shoes. I didn't mean to be late for dinner...'"

In the stage lights, his eyes take on the color of strong tea. He doesn't stumble over his words. In fact, he sounds like he reads aloud often.

"That was great," I say when he's done. But would he have chemistry with Sonata? Would people believe they were married?

"Thanks." Mica ducks his head as if he isn't used to taking compliments.

"Can you read it again, but this time imagine that your wife has just thrown one of her fuzzy slippers at you for no apparent reason?" I hold my breath, hoping for magic.

"Uh, okay."

Mica repeats the lines.

This time, his voice is full of doubt. His eyebrows pull together. He looks confused.

My heart thrums. I catch a glimmer of Martin Wright, Sylvia's husband in the play.

"Thanks for auditioning." I break into a smile, resisting the urge to offer Mica the part right away. I'm supposed to negotiate with the other directors for actors. Still, I have a good chance of casting him, since they'll want the more attractive male actors.

Ratna auditions next—I didn't know she was on the list. She's not bad, although she's obviously more comfortable writing than performing.

After Ratna leaves, I ponder who I could cast as the Star. I want her to be blond and impish, like Tinkerbell. Ashley, another actor who sometimes works with Lorna, might be good.

Then Sonata walks in. Her straight, dark brown hair tumbles down her back. Her olive skin glistens under the lights. She claims the stage with each step. I'm already impressed.

It's Lorna's turn to direct. Her play, titled *Please, Mr. Bank Manager, Save My Mother*, is about two sisters who attempt to rob a bank to get money for their mother's cancer treatments.

"'Put your hands up and no one gets hurt...'" Sonata begins.

She seems to make eye contact with every one of us. Her posture is flawless. She speaks like she means to gun us down. By the end of her monologue, I'm ready to fork over money for her fictional mother's treatments.

I catch my breath. She's perfect. I have to cast her as Sylvia. But Lorna's sure to want her, and maybe the other directors will too. What to do?

Sonata heads offstage. I stand, knocking my chair over with a loud thud. "Can you do evening rehearsals?" I blurt out.

"Pardon?" Sonata pivots on one foot like a dancer, squinting against the stage lights.

"Briar!" Lorna's eyes are hot coals.

My blood pulses faster. "Because I'd love you to play the lead in *Wish Upon a Star*." I fumble in my bag. "If you'd just read it, I promise you'll want the role." I jog closer, holding out the script.

Sonata's eyes find Lorna's before she extends a long-fingered hand to take the script. "Bold move." She smiles. "I like that." Then she exits stage right.

I hurry back to my seat. Samuel is laughing at Lorna's pinched face. A few others are frowning.

"That was amateur." Lorna turns on me, nostrils flaring. She looks me up and down, as if seeing me for the first time. "Why are you wearing those stupid glasses, anyway?"

"Because I can." I right my chair and take a seat, my heart pounding.

Three

Monday at lunchtime. A medieval jousting field. (At least, you could picture it that way.)

The seven Fringe directors stand on either side of the table, ready to battle it out for the actors they want to cast. Mr. Ty should be at the head of the table as judge, but he refuses to attend because he wants us to work it out ourselves. Lorna is facing me down. I'm glaring right back. Between us is a large chart listing all the plays and actors.

"I want to cast Sonata, Mica and Ashley." I talk loudly enough to be heard over the bickering of the other directors, their voices thick with their own arguments.

Across the table, Lorna comes back at me, full throttle. "You can't have Sonata or Ashley." She leans in. "I'm casting them."

I imagine Lorna lowering her visor and urging her horse into a gallop, her jousting lance aimed at my head.

"Sonata wants to be in my play," I say, my palms slick with sweat. "She told me so."

"She didn't say that!" Lorna's voice trembles. I picture her lance slipping out of her hands.

"She found me after media studies and told me that she loves the script. It 'speaks to her', she said."

Lorna's face goes scarlet. Her lance crashes to the ground. "It doesn't matter what Sonata wants. Mr. Ty will settle this." She spins on her heel and marches into the hall.

I follow, breathless. What if Mr. Ty sides with Lorna?

When someone grabs at my shoulder, I jump.

"Whoa, Briar. Calm down." Samuel raises his hands. "I just wanted to warn you—"

"About what?" I snap. My stomach is a mess of knots.

"I'm not sure you want Sarah in your cast."
He flips his long hair away from his face as if he
expects me to admire it.

I stare at him, confused. "You mean Sonata?"

He rolls his eyes. "I mean Sarah—that's what
she was in middle school, before she changed her
name and got so full of herself. I'm just saying...
you may not be glad to get her."

"Thanks for the warning, Samuel." I hurry to
catch up with Lorna, my shoes squeaking. I don't
want her to get to Mr. Ty first.

"I'm not kidding, Briar." Samuel's voice echoes
down the empty hallway. "Why do you think
most of the directors don't want to cast her?"

I pick up my pace.

Because they can't handle her, I think.

* * *

*Mr. Ty's office. Minutes later. Several half-
drunk mugs of coffee, piles of scripts, a papier-
mâché rhinoceros head and some pirate hats
clutter the room. Posters of Shakespeare and
past school performances decorate the walls.*

Lorna is already yammering to Mr. Ty. "Not only have I had to endure two days of auditions and callbacks with a bunch of amateurs, Briar doesn't even know how to negotiate for actors! She gave Sonata her script and begged her to take the lead! Like it's up to Sonata?" Lorna stomps her foot. Her eyes blaze. "Is Sonata suddenly a director?"

Mr. Ty swivels in his chair, his hands flat on the desk, his calm dark eyes flitting between us, his straight black hair gelled into spikes. "Lorna," he begins, his tone soothing, "you know I'm more of a learning coach than a teacher. I prefer to nurture independent thought in my students rather than dictate solutions."

Lorna hardly takes a breath. "You have to settle this, Mr. Ty. Briar is trying to take two of my actors—Sonata and Ashley—and everyone knows that they always work with me. I wrote this play with them in mind. They're perfect for the roles—"

"Didn't you ask me to settle a dispute between you and Sonata during last year's Fringe?"

Lorna gapes. "Yes—I mean, no. It wasn't a dispute. It was a...misunderstanding."

"I recall that Sonata refused to follow your stage directions and you asked for help." Mr. Ty turns to me. "I see nothing wrong with sharing a script with an actor."

Lorna gasps. I straighten my shoulders.

Mr. Ty continues. "Why don't you tell me about your casting plans, Briar?"

I wipe my sweaty palms on my jeans and explain how I like the physical differences between Sonata and Mica, and how blond, waif-like Ashley is a perfect fit as the Star.

"Interesting ideas." Mr. Ty nods. "Briar, did you try to work this out with Lorna?"

"Of course," I say. "We talked in the directors' meeting. Lorna says I can't have either actor." I try to sound level-headed. What if I don't get Sonata and Ashley?

"Yes, and you've come to me for a ruling." Mr. Ty strikes a regal pose and waves an imaginary scepter. "Well, if I must..." He pauses to study Lorna and then me, lingering on my red cat's-eye frames. "Sonata will work with Briar this year."

A weight lifts off my chest.

"What?" Lorna's voice breaks. "Why?"

Mr. Ty raises one finger. "Because you directed her last year." He raises another. "Because you two have a history of conflict."

"But Mr. Ty, you said that casting is eighty percent of the play's interpretation, so I need to choose actors who are right for my vision." Lorna's fingers are clenched. "Maybe Sonata could do both plays?"

"Impossible. Performances start May eighth— that's just over four weeks away. You and Briar will both be scheduling rehearsals before and after school. And Sonata will have her classwork to complete as well."

"What about Ashley?" Lorna pleads.

"You will cast Ashley." He gives Lorna a somber look. "Let's hope she's a better fit for you."

"But Mr. Ty," I say, feeling the panic rise in my gut, "I planned for my Star character to be female, and I doubt there are any female actors left, since the other directors—"

"Casting is a balance between the ideal and the real, Briar. Any director needs to make compromises." Mr. Ty sips from one of his coffee mugs.

"But how—" I begin.

"Change your director's vision. Play a male actor in a female role," Mr. Ty says. "Either way, you need to make this work."

There's no point in arguing. I nod. "Thanks, Mr. Ty," I say before racing Lorna back to the directors' meeting to find myself a Star.

Four

The main-floor girls' bathroom at Whitlock.
Wednesday after school. A tap drips.

Ratna is planted in front of the row of
mirrors, anxiously smoothing her hair for
the tenth time.

"Hurry. I can't be late." I bounce on my toes,
my director's binder under my arm. On the cover,
I've painted a silver star. Inside are my dreams
for *Wish Upon a Star*—songs that inspired me,
character research, lighting and costume ideas
and a copy of the play, of course. I can't wait to
get started.

"What have you heard about Lorna as a director?"
Ratna spins to face me. "What if she doesn't like my
acting? What if I'm not good enough?"

"I've heard she's tough but her performances are good. And you've taken two years of drama at Whitlock, so you can't be bad."

"But so has everyone else." Her voice rises. "Sonata even did four commercials this year. She's already a professional!"

"If Lorna cast you, then she must like your acting." Ratna doesn't know she was one of the last picks, and I'm not about to tell her.

"Maybe Lorna had to take me. You had to cast Clayton as your Star when you didn't want to."

"Don't remind me." I make a face, remembering how I tried to trade Clayton for any other actor, including Ratna, with no luck. "I'm making the best of it. Anyway, Clayton isn't in the same category as you. You have an expressive face and voice."

In the directors' meeting, I couldn't remember who Clayton was until Samuel described him. Clayton had read flat in audition, as if he didn't care. Also, he was short, maybe five foot five, with brown skin, scruffy facial hair and cropped black curls. Not quite the Tinkerbell vision I was going for.

I take Ratna by the shoulders and make her look me in the eyes. "Listen to me. You'll be great.

The bank teller is a small role—you don't need to talk much." When Ratna gets stage fright, her voice comes out in a squeak. "I know you can do this."

Ratna's dark eyes are watery. "Okay. Let's go."

We walk down the hall—past a swarm of dancers in bodysuits and a guy carrying a tuba case—and turn toward the cafeteria. Mr. Ty has reserved it for all Fringe Festival directors every day after school, if we need it. I'm hoping to book one of the smaller drama rooms for some of my rehearsals, but for the read-through, the cafeteria will do.

"The first reading is so important." I grip my binder against my chest, feeling more jumpy with each step. "It's the actors' first impression of the play."

Ratna gives me a sympathetic look. "I know you can do this." She's repeating my words, even using the same tone of voice.

I frown. "I just want them to feel inspired when they read *Wish Upon a Star* together for the first time. I want them to feel excited about my staging ideas."

"I could always help you with ideas, if you want."

"I'm fine," I say, even though I'm tempted to tell her to back off. I'm the director and she's the writer. Her ideas are already in the script. It's my turn now. "Let's just go do our read-throughs."

* * *

Whitlock cafeteria. A few minutes later. A row of windows overlooks a city street. The tables and benches have been pushed to one side. The doors to the kitchen are closed and locked.

Mr. Ty is at a table, handing out copies of scripts. Directors, actors and stage managers gather in clumps, chatting excitedly.

Ratna joins Lorna, Ashley and the rest of her cast, who are already reading from *Please, Mr. Bank Manager, Save My Mother*. Near the windows, Samuel's actors laugh loudly at something he said.

Meanwhile, Clayton slouches against a table, busy with his phone, his back to Mica. Sonata rushes in, still wearing her dance tights and bodysuit—she's in the Whitlock Spring Dance Show next week. Mica gazes at Sonata like she's a goddess. My assigned stage manager, George Kostas, is nowhere in sight.

I should have guessed this would happen. George, whom I've known since grade six, has good intentions, but he's easily distracted.

I rush to collect copies of my script from Mr. Ty, which is supposed to be George's job.

When I tell Mr. Ty about George, he says, "You'll need to keep a close eye on your stage manager."

I'm flustered and off-balance. This is not how I imagined my read-through.

I gather my actors in a circle of chairs near the only unoccupied corner—beside the recycling and garbage bins. Voices echo off the tile floor. Sonata turns up her nose at the smell of rotting food.

I straighten my glasses and then start with the welcome speech I practiced last night in my bedroom.

"Acting is a kind of magic," I say. "It can make the audience laugh and cry. It can reveal the truth about the world."

Clayton yawns and examines his black high-tops. Sonata's back is perfectly straight, her hands folded in her lap, her gaze intense.

Mica edges his chair closer to her, his pudgy stomach pushing against his T-shirt.

My speech sounded more inspiring last night. "I'm thrilled to be directing you in *Wish Upon a Star*. I know we can bring the audience to its feet."

I pass out the copies of the script. They thumb through them.

"Before we read, I want to share with you my vision for the play. *Wish Upon a Star* is a comedy that takes place in Martin and Sylvia Wright's kitchen." I nod toward Mica and Sonata.

Mica's eyes slide off Sonata and onto me. Sonata smiles steadily.

"A kitchen is the heart of a home—it can reveal a lot about the people who live there. Martin and Sylvia's kitchen will be staged in gaudy, mismatched colors that symbolize their divided marriage. I want to contrast this with the glitter and natural beauty of a Star." I point to Clayton, who raises his thick eyebrows. "Our Star symbolizes the hope that wishes bring—the hope that Sylvia has for her future."

"Yeah, I don't know about glitter." Clayton lifts his stubbly chin, his eyes cold.

"Don't you think a mismatched kitchen is too obvious?" Sonata flips her hair over one shoulder. "Maybe it should be shades of pink? I think it's Sylvia's favorite color."

I bite my tongue. I remember the dozens of times I've read the play, analyzing the plot, characters, dialogue, setting and theme. It took me days to come up with my vision. "That's an interesting idea, Sonata, but I'll handle the—"

"What if we—" Sonata begins.

"Let's just read through the play." I paste on a smile. "Don't worry about the details now." I flip to the first page of the script in my binder and read the opening stage directions out loud—another of George's jobs. "'SETTING. The kitchen of Martin and Sylvia Wright. AT RISE, Sylvia stands before a sink full of dirty dishes, staring out the window. It's late evening. Martin sits alone at the kitchen table, eating.'"

"'The stars are out tonight,'" Sonata begins.

Her voice has a tremor in it—she has good instincts. When Mica speaks, his every word oozes infatuation—not exactly in character for a neglectful husband. Clayton drones his lines.

I stare hard through my glasses at my script, fighting the urge to correct my actors, telling myself to wait for rehearsals, when I can give each performer detailed director notes about how to play the character. We have a long way to go in only four weeks.

Fifteen minutes later, we're only halfway through, but two other groups are already finishing up.

Mr. Ty stands on a table to get our attention.

"Before the room empties," he says, "I have an announcement that will interest many of you." He pauses dramatically.

The room goes quiet.

"Next month, Whitlock will have two new extracurricular workshops—one in acting and one in directing. We've asked a top acting coach and a professional director to lead these workshops, which will be by invitation only for students who show exceptional promise."

The room fills with noise. My heart thuds. How can I get into that directing workshop?

"Will we get extra performance opportunities?" Sonata takes a step toward Mr. Ty.

"What do we have to do to get in?" Samuel says.

"Is it for senior students only?" Lorna pushes in front of him.

"Any student may be invited to attend, and a stunning Fringe performance won't hurt your chances." Mr. Ty jumps off the table and is instantly surrounded.

My actors bolt toward the mob.

"Wait!" I call. How am I going to create a stunning performance with this cast? "All lines need to be memorized in two weeks. We'll have rehearsals three times a week, after school for two hours, starting tomorrow. If we want to do this right, we need to—"

Before I can finish, they've disappeared into the crowd.

Five

Briar's bedroom. Later that day. A single bed with a purple IKEA duvet. Over the bed, playbills from theater performances cover one wall and part of the next—The Tempest, War Horse, photocopied playbills from local community theaters, last year's Whitlock Fringe Festival poster.

Ratna flops down on my bed. "I still can't believe you've seen all these shows!" We've been friends for over a year, but she's only been to my house once. We're both too busy with school events.

I drop my backpack on the floor, still thinking about the directing workshop Mr. Ty just announced. "My aunt Darla took me to most of them.

My first one was when I was six." I point to a playbill from *King Lear*. "Not a play for kids, considering Gloucester gets his eyes gouged out and Lear goes crazy before he dies. But I loved it."

"Wow! At six, I was watching Disney's *Cinderella*."

Darla glides into the room, wearing a multi-colored peasant dress and a jean jacket. "Disney perpetuates the myth that marriage is all life has to offer a girl."

Ratna giggles. "You mean there's more?"

"How's the new job, Darla?" I say, to distract her from her usual anti-Disney rant. If she keeps this job for more than a few weeks, she'll likely move out again, which will cut down on the number of arguments at mealtimes.

"They don't understand that time is flexible." She sighs. "Nine AM is such an arbitrary hour to start work."

"We have to be at school by nine," I point out. Sometimes I wonder if Darla and Mom are really sisters—they're so different. Maybe it's because Mom is ten years older.

"Exactly," Darla says, like I've agreed with her. "What's wrong with arriving at noon? Or working at midnight? As long as I put in the time—" She stops suddenly and examines my glasses. "Cool frames. No lenses?" She nods. "Very symbolic."

"Yup." I take off my glasses and toss them on my desk. I love how free-spirited my aunt is, but I don't want to bond with her over my glasses. Maybe because it took her a week to even notice them. Maybe because, unlike her, I'm going to have a successful career in the theater—starting with *Wish Upon a Star* and a spot in Mr. Ty's directing workshop.

"We have work to do." I interrupt Darla, who's starting in on Disney again. "Come on, Ratna. I'll help you memorize your lines."

*   *   *

A main-floor drama room at Whitlock. Two days later, after school. Black wooden boxes arranged strategically on the raised staging area. The curtains pulled back. Dim lights where the audience will sit.

"This is our stage for Fringe Festival." I step into a cascade of stage lighting and smile down at

Sonata, Mica, Clayton and George, who'd promised to attend after I yelled at him in English class. "We won't always be able to rehearse in here, but I managed to book it for our first rehearsal."

Sonata eyes my set structure critically, while Mica gazes at her and Clayton picks at his nails. George has the prompt book open on his lap. I think he may be doodling in the script, which I try to ignore.

"Here"—I point stage left to a large box with four smaller ones around it—"is where we'll place the kitchen table and chairs. And here"—I motion stage right to an even row of waist-high boxes—"will be the counter and sink. The window will be above the sink, and our Star can enter stage right." I walk downstage toward them. "I hope to dig up a fifties-style table and chairs from the props room and maybe even some sort of sink and window. But this gives you a rough idea of the set structure."

I step off the low stage, hoping to hear how brilliant my plan is.

"Why not aim the window toward the audience so they can see me when I stare out at the stars?" Sonata stands, towering over me. A crease forms between her delicate eyebrows.

Mica nods. "They'll want to see Sonata's face. It's so expressive."

George continues drawing in the prompt book.

I frown. Sonata may be right, but I can't let her boss me around. "No. The set will block the action." I ponder arranging the counter and sink at an angle to the audience.

The crease in Sonata's forehead deepens. "I accepted a role in this play because I thought you'd listen to feedback."

What the hell? I square my shoulders. "All I want is for you to play your part, Sonata, so that I can direct."

"Briar, you have to understand that I have a lot at stake right now." Her voice starts to waver, and I wonder if she's acting. "I need this performance to go well."

"We all do." I set my jaw. "It will be fine." Obviously, she wants a spot in the exclusive acting workshop. Or maybe it's because she's graduating this year. Ratna says she's applying to all the top acting schools.

"Fine isn't good enough." Sonata sniffs. "It has to be perfect."

"It'll be better than perfect." Are the tears in her eyes real or forced?

"Hey, Briar," Clayton says. "While we're talking, I've got to tell you that the glitter is no good. In fact, I think this part may not be right for me—"

"Don't interrupt, Clayton." Mica elbows him. "Sonata's talking to Briar."

"I'll interrupt anyone I want to." Clayton narrows his eyes at Mica, who backs down, even though he's four inches taller and twice as wide.

My stomach flutters. I need to take control. "Let's just warm up with an improv game," I say.

"You're a fabulous actor." Mica leans closer to Sonata, who looks at him, startled. "I feel like I have a lot to learn from you."

"Mica!" I yell. "We're trying to rehearse!"

George glances up from the prompt book. Mica's jaw drops. Sonata raises a hand to her mouth. Clayton smirks.

I sit on the edge of the stage and put my head in my hands. I blew it. No matter what happens, a director should stay calm. I'm acting like an amateur.

I take a deep breath. "Look, we all want to create the greatest possible experience for the audience. Right?"

Sonata and Mica nod.

George returns to the prompt book.

Clayton looks skeptical.

"We can do that best by working together." I rise to my feet, ready to take charge no matter who does what. "George, please write up a rehearsal schedule and email it to everyone. The rest of you, let's do some improv. Who knows Hot Seat? You know—when we take turns asking one actor questions to answer in character?"

"Everyone knows Hot Seat." Sonata sounds offended.

"Great." I collapse into one of the audience chairs near George. "You can go first, Sonata."

My actors meander onto the stage and sit around my makeshift table. Sonata's eyes are glassy and distant. Mica looks wounded. Clayton slouches.

I push my glasses up higher on my nose, trying not to feel like I'm a lousy director.

"Sylvia," I address Sonata's character, "tell me how you first met Martin."

Her facial features rearrange until Sonata becomes a falsely cheerful Sylvia. Incredible.

"We met in high school," she begins, her voice projecting into the audience. "Martin sat behind me in biology. I always knew he had a crush on me. He was voted most likely to be a workaholic. I was voted most likely to keep my figure."

Six

A French class at Whitlock. Monday morning.

Madame Bouchard writes a new assignment on the whiteboard—an oral speech to be written, memorized and presented in seven days.

The class groans.

I grip my pencil tighter. I don't have time for this assignment. Or the math test on Friday. Or my science lab. Rehearsals matter more. And I need to locate my set pieces and props, find someone to be my lighting and sound tech, look for costumes, keep George on track.

My right leg develops a nervous tremble. I wrap it around the leg of my desk to keep it still.

When my cell phone vibrates in my pocket, I don't even notice it at first.

I check my phone when Madame Bouchard's back is turned. It's a text from Sonata.

Can't make rehearsal 2nite. Extra rehearsal for dance show. Sorry.

Our second rehearsal, with just over three weeks to opening night, and she can't come?

The quiver in my leg gets stronger. Martin and the Star don't even have any scenes together. How will I run a rehearsal?

Madame Bouchard turns around, almost catching me with my phone out.

I slip it into my desk and try to pay attention.

But all I can think about is Sonata and her stupid dance show.

Rehearsals are nothing without her.

*   *   *

The set and prop room. Same day at lunch. Floor-to-ceiling shelves are stacked with large clear plastic boxes with weird labels. CUPS AND GOBLETS. WOODEN DAGGERS. CANDLESTICKS.

PAPER MONEY and COINS. Beyond the shelves is the furniture.

Mr. Ty lets only a few Fringe directors and their stage managers in at once. I get stuck with Lorna and Samuel and their sidekicks. George is nowhere to be seen, but at least I'll get the set and props done right.

While the others argue over who gets which plastic guns, I rummage through a bin of fake food until I find a basket of strawberries and something that resembles burnt steak. I'm glad mine is the only play set in a kitchen.

After I locate a few dishes with gaudy flowers, some mismatched cutlery and an old metal pot, I go searching for my sink and table.

Furniture and large props are stacked impossibly high. There are oversized flowers from a musical version of *Alice in Wonderland*, a throne painted gold, three couches from different time periods and Victorian chairs. I could spend days in here, just poking around.

Several Greek columns lean into a corner. Two enormous tragedy and comedy masks hang on one wall. A metal chicken coop sits on sections of a white picket fence.

I climb over about forty plastic pink flamingos—left over from the graduation prank last year—to find a fifties-style table with chrome legs. Perfect.

As I'm searching for a sink, my phone buzzes again. This time it's Clayton, making some stupid excuse for why he has to miss tonight's rehearsal. I sigh. How can I run through a scene with one actor?

"What's wrong?" Samuel appears from behind the shelves, without his stage manager. "Can't find your props?"

"Props are the easy part." I hold up my burnt steak. "They're more agreeable than actors." The words slip out before I can stop them. I don't want Samuel to think that I can't handle things or that I need advice. I get enough advice from Sonata, Lorna and even Ratna.

But Samuel just laughs. "Tell me about it." He runs his fingers through his hair and examines me with a sly smile.

Is he flirting with me?

I back away, stumbling over a few pink flamingos. "See you later," I mumble. Romance is the last thing I need.

"You bet."

When I glance back, Samuel is still watching me.

* * *

Whitlock cafeteria. Later that day. The room has been transformed into a rehearsal studio. Scripts lie open on the floor. Backpacks have been tossed against the walls. A few odd props are stacked on tables.

In the middle of the room, directors, actors and stage managers have gathered for a warm-up game of Battle-Axe while Mr. Ty looks on. It's one of my favorite games, but I don't feel like joining in.

The game is simple. Everyone stands in a giant circle, and one person begins by throwing an imaginary battle-axe at another person with a guttural cry. The second person catches the axe and throws it again. It can be fun to get several axes going around the circle—some small and some massive.

I'm not surprised to see George playing with gusto, his ears sticking out comically, his freckled face red as he bellows and throws an axe.

Mica is there too, tossing with less effort, his face shining and happy.

I lean against a table until they're done, avoiding Mr. Ty because I don't want him to notice that I can't even get my actors to come to rehearsal. Mica beams as he approaches me. George's face is still flushed.

George and I run lines with Mica, which is all we can do. When I comment on Mica's cheerful mood, he tells me that Sonata has promised to go for coffee with him—maybe next week.

"I think she's into me." He smiles.

"Oh," I say, wondering if Sonata really does like him. "Great news." I can't help worrying about what a date will do to their stage dynamics.

I watch Ratna laughing and talking with Lorna, Ashley and the other actors in their play. Lorna puts an arm around Ratna's shoulder, chatting while Ratna nods eagerly. Samuel's actors seem to have most of their lines memorized already.

It's depressing.

I end rehearsal early and walk home alone.

* * *

Briar's kitchen. Late evening.

Dad is warming milk on the stove. He has the *Financial Times* tucked under one arm.

I rummage through the kitchen drawers in search of Mom's stash of aprons. Although she rarely wears them, I remember a colorful one from Darla that would work for Sylvia.

"Dad..." I sit back on my heels. "How do you get people on a team to listen—people who have to work together?" He doesn't know anything about theater, but I've heard him talk about managing teams at work.

"Well"—Dad leans against the stove—"I explain logically what needs to be done and why."

"That only works if people are highly motivated," Mom says behind me. "Sometimes you need to tell them what to do."

Both Mom and Darla have come into the kitchen—not good. Mom is in a linen suit, while Darla wears jeans with rips at the knees and a Bob Marley T-shirt.

"That never works." Darla gives Mom an incredulous look. "You need to inspire them, even though it's against my principles to force people to listen in the first place. Why not let them think for themselves?"

"Do your principles include paying for room and board?" Dad asks.

Mom frowns at him. "Don't start."

But it's too late.

As the shouting begins, I head upstairs to my room and shut the door. So much for teamwork. I'll find an apron later.

Seven

Whitlock cafeteria. Two days later, after school. The din of seven sets of directors, actors and stage managers echoes throughout the room.

Mica and Clayton wait beside our staging area for their cues. The recycling bins stand stage right, acting as our makeshift sink and counter. Four stackable plastic chairs sit stage left, around a nonexistent table. Sonata plunges her hands into the imaginary dishwater and pretends to wash a plate. She stares dreamily out the "window" and up at the "stars," her lips slightly parted.

"'Star light, star bright...'" she begins.

My shoulders are tight, and my neck aches. "Pay attention," I whisper to George, beside me.

He's laughing at Samuel's play—a comedy about a love triangle gone bad—instead of writing my actors' blocking cues in our prompt book.

"Great, Sonata," I say when she finishes her wish and returns to washing dishes, her eyes overbright. "Now, Clayton, you're going to enter upstage of Sylvia, who will turn toward you. Do you have that written down, George?" I glare at him, wishing I could will him into being the perfect stage manager.

"Huh?" George looks startled, a grin still lurking on his face as one of Samuel's actors tosses fake rose petals about their staging area.

"Briar." Sonata whacks her script against her thigh. "I can't possibly turn my back to the audience at this crucial moment."

I grit my teeth. Not again. "Yes, you can, Sonata. It's only for a moment. Because as our Star walks downstage, you'll spin to open to the audience."

Sonata winces. "Sylvia's reaction to the Star should be seen."

"It will be seen. But first the audience needs to see the Star, so we give him the stage and then we show Sylvia's reaction."

"But, Briar—"

"Sonata, please, will you just let me do my job?" My hands are clenched. I try to relax them.

Sonata folds her arms across her chest and hugs herself. Is she really that upset?

"I think Sonata—" Mica begins.

"Not now, Mica." I turn to George. "Did you write down Clayton's cue?"

George ignores me.

I smack him on the shoulder.

He jumps. "What?"

"Write down Clayton's cue." I emphasize each syllable.

"Fine." He sneaks a peek at Samuel's actors again. "What is it?"

"Enter upstage right."

"He's just going to walk in?" George's eyebrows shoot up.

Now George is questioning me? "Of course he's going to walk in. What else would he do?"

George shrugs. "I thought he would fly."

"Cool," Clayton says.

"That could work." Sonata nods.

"I like it too." Mica agrees with her, of course.

My face heats up. "The Star can't fly through our window. It'll be too small. And how would we get him to fly, anyway? No. He'll land outside the house—offstage—and then walk in."

"Through the door?" George snorts. "That's boring."

"Could you just write down the cue?" I shout. Lorna and a few others gape at us.

"Whatever." He scribbles something in the prompt script and returns to watching Samuel's play.

I sigh. "Clayton, you're on now. Sonata, you turn upstage as he enters."

Clayton steps onto our staging area, looking uncomfortable. Sonata refuses to follow my directions, keeping her face to the audience as he walks downstage.

My head pounds. "Next time, we'll need Sylvia to face upstage"—I'm careful to control my tone of voice—"but let's move on for now. We'll have some theme music for the Star's entrance. I'm still deciding what that will be. And the lighting will make him seem to shimmer. Go ahead with your line, Sonata."

"'You're...you're glowing!'" Sonata says to the Star. "'Who are you?'"

Clayton reads from his script in a wooden voice, one word at a time. "'I...am...a...Star.'"

"'You heard my wish?'" Sonata falls to her knees.

Clayton squints at his script. "'We...all...did...'" He stumbles over his words, not even trying.

"Clayton, you should have learned some of your lines by now!" I can't stand his bumbling any longer.

"Yeah, I can't get into these lines. They're just not me." He drops his script.

"No, they're the Star's lines. Maybe if you'd memorize them, you'd see that. George, why don't you run lines with Clayton while I work with Sonata and Mica? George? George!"

After I get George's attention, I set him up at a nearby table with Clayton and a script. When I return to our makeshift stage, it's pretty obvious that Mica is begging Sonata for a date.

"How about tomorrow night?" He steps closer.

"I have dance practice." Sonata shakes her head, looking disappointed. Does she really want to go out with him? Or is she trying to let him down easy?

"Plan it later, guys." I frown. "We need to rehearse."

Then I catch sight of Lorna watching me, a smirk on her face. I try not to notice how organized her rehearsal is. Even Ratna seems relaxed and happy.

"I'm free Friday night," Mica pleads.

"That's the dance show." Sonata flips her hair over one shoulder.

I straighten my glasses and focus on Sonata and Mica. "I said, plan it later!" I've raised my voice. My rehearsal must look pathetic.

Sonata purses her lips. Mica retreats. I'm just relieved they listened.

"Let's review your first scene together, before Sylvia's wish," I say. "The blocking is fine, but I'd like to work on Mica's reactions. How do you think Martin feels when Sylvia throws a slipper at him?"

"Uh, surprised?" Mica gazes at Sonata as if he's hoping for approval.

Sonata nods encouragingly. Who's the director here?

"Yes, and maybe he feels a little confused too," I say. "Let's try it again."

Sonata takes her position for the scene. Mica's eyes follow her.

"'You want to know what's for dinner?'" She pretends to remove a slipper and lob it at Mica. "'Here's the chef's special!'"

Sonata turns into Sylvia in the blink of an eye. If I weren't so frustrated with her, I could enjoy her acting more.

"'You hired a chef?'" Mica's voice drips with affection and longing.

"Mica, I'm still reading infatuation, not confusion," I say.

"I'm trying my best." Mica shoves his hands deep into his pockets.

"Yes, and you're doing fine. Let's do it again, this time with a neutral face and no expression, just for kicks." I'm hoping we can start with no emotion and then build to Martin's feelings.

"'You hired a chef?'" Mica repeats. This time, he pastes on a deadpan expression, although his voice gives away his desire for Sonata.

I attempt a smile. "Let's try that one more time." I glance at George and Clayton, who are laughing and talking over the script. Could they actually be working?

I work with Sonata and Mica until the end of rehearsal, trying and failing to help Mica get in character, writing the blocking cues in our prompt book myself and giving director notes that my actors continue to ignore. As everyone leaves, I consider talking to Mr. Ty about how to control my cast, but he's chatting with Lorna.

I shove the chairs and recycling bins back in place, stalling for time, hoping Lorna will go, even though I'm not sure what to say to Mr. Ty. *I can't get Mica to show any emotion except infatuation? Sonata won't stop directing? Clayton won't learn his lines? George won't do anything?*

Mr. Ty will think I'm a failure.

Forget it. I hoist my backpack and head out. As I pass Mr. Ty and Lorna, I hear him say, "A successful director empowers actors to create great art as a team."

"That's so true!" Lorna fake-smiles at me.

I step into the hall, where Ratna's waiting for me. Am I a successful director?

Right now, I can't seem to empower anyone, especially myself.

Eight

Bean Me Up coffee shop, three blocks from Whitlock. A week later at lunchtime. A wobbly table that's too uneven to set a drink on. Uncomfortable chairs designed to make you leave quickly. The scent of roasting coffee.

Ratna and I sit near the front window, cupping our mugs and staring through the steamed-up windows at the spring rain. My glasses are perched on top of my head. After another week of challenging rehearsals crammed between mountains of homework, I want a break from thinking like a director. If only Ratna would stop ranting about Lorna's terrific rehearsals.

"And then Lorna says that she doesn't want to tell me *how* to act—that I should bring my own ideas to the scene." Ratna breaks off a chunk of cranberry muffin and pops it in her mouth, chewing happily.

"She never gives advice?" I snort. Lorna loves to offer me "friendly advice" when she's really telling me what to do.

"Well..." Ratna finishes chewing. "She gives examples of how to act, and she reminds us what the script says." She rips apart her muffin, tearing the tender inside into bite-sized pieces. "It's going well—we've got the whole play blocked, and now we're working on gestures that show character motivation."

"Yeah?" I nibble my bagel, wishing I could get to that point with my actors.

Ratna smiles. "Yup. The bank teller's hands shake whenever the sisters aim a gun at her. She's thinking how she wants to make it home to her son."

I frown. It's a good motivation. I bet Lorna thought of it.

Ratna studies my face. "Maybe you should talk to Lorna. She might be able to help with—"

"No. I'm fine." I lean back in my chair and glance away. There's a line of people at the counter, waiting to order—mostly Whitlock students. I can't bear to think about which of them will come to see my play and whether it'll even be worth watching.

"Okay." Ratna gives me an anxious look. "It was just an idea."

A bad idea. I imagine Lorna's snooty expression as she tells me how wrong my approach is. I frown and start to drum my fingers on the table just as Sonata pushes through the line of people. She's coming from the back of the café and racing toward the exit. Her face is pale with red splotches, her eyes darting.

"Sonata?" I stand, shoving my chair back. "Are you okay?"

Her eyes barely focus as she hurries past without answering. Long strands of dark hair cling to her cheeks.

"What was that about?" Ratna gapes.

"I have no idea," I say, realizing how little I know about Sonata's life outside school. "She's been really busy with the spring dance show, but now that it's over I thought she'd calm down."

I'm about to follow her out—offer to help somehow, even though it's none of my business unless it affects rehearsals—when Mica pushes through the same crowd, following Sonata.

"Mica?" I wave him over. "Were you with Sonata? What's going on?"

Mica looks dazed. He wipes a meaty hand over his face. "Why doesn't she want to date me?" His bottom lip quivers. "After I finally got her out for coffee. What's wrong with me?"

He takes off into the rain.

"Wait!" I glance at Ratna, who's staring after Mica. So are most of the customers. "I should try to do something," I say. "Sorry."

"Of course. Go." She nods, her eyes still wide.

"Thanks. I'll talk to you later."

I shove the rest of my bagel in my bag, dart outside and hurry toward the school. The rain starts hammering. I pull up the hood of my Whitlock sweatshirt and scan the sidewalk for Sonata and Mica, who are nowhere in sight.

As I break into a run, my glasses slide down my forehead and land on the tip of my nose. I nudge them up into place, wondering what this mess is going to do to Sonata and Mica's stage chemistry. I reach the school in time to see Sonata disappearing inside. Maybe Mica took off somewhere else.

I step into the main foyer and shake off the rain. Near the fashion class's display of mannequins in duct-tape dresses, Lorna is comforting Sonata, her arms wrapped around her as they whisper together.

I take a step forward, not sure what to do. Sure, Mica was pressuring Sonata, but I couldn't tell if she liked the attention. Should I have interfered?

Lorna's eyes meet mine and then narrow.

I'm so not wanted.

I head for my locker, still soggy, wondering how to handle the next rehearsal with two emotionally fragile actors. What am I going to say to them? I cringe just thinking about it.

"Briar!" someone calls. "I've been looking for you."

I turn to find George rushing toward me.

"Hey, George," I say, hoping he's not bringing me more problems to handle.

"Come with me." He latches onto my arm and tugs me back the way I came. "I've got a surprise for you."

Not what I expected. "Where are we going?" I yank my arm free but keep walking.

"The main-floor drama room. Hurry. Clayton's waiting."

"Clayton? What's this about?"

He grins, and his sticking-out ears go red. "Can't tell you, but you're going to love it!"

I stare at George. Why is he so excited?

As we pass through the foyer, George calls to Sonata, "You've got to see this too! Come on."

Sonata dabs at her eyes and follows us. Unfortunately, so does Lorna.

"What's up?" Lorna asks.

"You'll see." George turns the corner and then stops abruptly by the door of the room where we'll be performing *Wish Upon a Star* in front of a live audience in only two short weeks.

"You're about to witness a spectacular feat of staging wizardry." He spreads his arms dramatically, catching the attention of a few others in the hall. "Come inside." He motions to the open classroom door.

We file into the dimmed room, and some onlookers from the hall trail after us. I peer into the shadows. The stage is set up in a rough version of our set, the curtains drawn back. I get a sick feeling in my stomach. Is George going to do something stupid?

"Wait here." George stops us in front of the set. "Ready, Clayton?" he calls.

"Ready!" Clayton says from somewhere stage right.

"George," I begin, "are you sure—"

"Relax, Briar." He turns to Sonata and the others. "At first we were trying to rig a cord to the lighting grid so Clayton could fly in, but we thought this would work better."

"Tell me you didn't!" I peer up at the thick rods that support the stage lights. Clayton's weight could tear the grid out of the ceiling.

"We didn't." George jogs over to the switch and flicks on the overhead lights.

I gasp when I see Clayton strapped into fifties-style roller skates, standing at the top of a ramp.

The room fills with noise as people urge Clayton on. Sonata clamps a hand over her mouth. Lorna gives me a look like this is my fault. Before I can do anything, Clayton pushes off.

He rolls down the ramp and is airborne briefly, arms windmilling, before he crashes face down on the stage.

We rush toward him.

"That was even better the second time, buddy!" George says.

"Are you okay?" I ask.

Clayton moans and rolls over. "My arm!" he gasps. His right forearm has an unnatural curve above the wrist, like the bones are painfully out of position.

"I think it's broken." Sonata's mascara is smudged.

"Why did you let him do that?" Lorna asks, turning to me.

My face heats up. "I didn't know," I say, even though the director is always supposed to be in charge.

"This play is cursed," Lorna says in a loud voice. "I don't know how you're ever going to stage it."

I want to sink through the floor and disappear.

Sonata flinches. "How could you say that?"

"I didn't mean you, Sonata." Lorna glares at me.

The bell rings for class.

Mr. Ty appears. "What happened here?"

Everyone answers at once. Mr. Ty's face clouds over. I can't bear the disappointment in his eyes.

Nine

Late evening. Briar's secret hideout. (At least, it used to be.)

T he front window in our living room has a wide ledge. When I was a kid, I'd drag old blankets and pillows onto it and shut the heavy curtains, pretending that I was backstage. I'd peek through the curtains at my parents reading in the living room or arguing with Darla, and I'd imagine they were part of a show that I'd staged. Behind me, the driveway, the birch tree in the front yard and the street beyond didn't exist. I was invisible in my secret hideout.

Tonight, I pull my knees up and hug a pillow to my chest. My hideout doesn't seem so secret anymore, especially when Mom waves to me as she parks her Jetta in the driveway.

In the kitchen, Dad's already making dinner. I can smell salmon and garlic and hear him setting the table, but I doubt I can eat. Not with this ache in my gut.

Clayton went to the hospital to get his arm set. Sonata was wound tighter than usual. Mica disappeared. Mr. Ty scolded George and then me—that was the worst. "You're responsible for the safety of the actors. I shouldn't have to tell you this." Afterward, George followed me around like a distressed puppy, guilty and eager to please. Maybe he'll do his job now. As if that will help.

I bite the inside of my cheek, wondering how I'm going to sort out the mess that is my play. Maybe Lorna was right. Maybe it *is* cursed. Maybe Mr. Ty has already ruled me out for the advanced directing workshop.

I stare at the curtains and ponder how to handle my next rehearsal. Dad said I should explain logically what needs to be done. Mom thinks I should tell people what to do. Darla said to inspire them. But Mica is too emotional to listen to reason, Sonata is too stubborn to take direction, and Clayton is hardly inspired. Then I remember that Mr. Ty said a successful director empowers actors. Is that what Lorna's been doing all along? Will it work for me? And how exactly do I do it?

I'm startled out of my thoughts when Mom draws back the living-room curtains. She's still in her work clothes—an ivory V-neck blouse and a black pencil skirt.

"What's wrong?" She feels my forehead. "Why are you hiding behind the curtains?"

I tuck my knees under my chin. My glasses sit beside me on the ledge. "It's nothing." As if Mom could understand.

"I bet it's that play she's working on." Darla appears behind Mom. Her hair is braided in corn-rows, with beads woven in. "Are you about two weeks from opening?"

I nod. How does Darla know? I haven't been talking about it much at home.

"That's always when everything goes to hell," Darla says. "It's perfectly normal. It has to go wrong so it can go right in the end."

"I'm not so sure," I say. "This play may be different."

"It's never different." Darla shakes her head and her beads click.

"You know what's always bothered me?" Mom snaps at Darla.

Darla lets out a long breath. "I know you're going to tell me."

"It bothers me that you always romanticize the theater in front of Briar." Mom's tone is sharp.

I get a heavy feeling in my chest. Not another fight.

"I'm not—" Darla begins.

"Yes, you are. Even though you're a guest in our home, you hold up your unsustainable artistic lifestyle like it's somehow better than ours. Glamorous. More exciting. But it hasn't done much for you. And I don't want Briar believing in it any more than I wanted you to believe in it."

I squeeze my eyes shut. Will this day never end?

Darla flips her beaded hair over one shoulder. "Just say it. You don't want Briar to be a failure like me—a wannabe actress who didn't make it."

"Your words, not mine." Mom's neck is rigid.

"Maybe I would have succeeded if I'd had support. Maybe you should be supporting Briar in whatever she chooses to do."

"We support you every time you lose your job." Dad enters from the kitchen, gesturing at the dining-room table set for four. "And we'll support our daughter too. We just want her to choose a sensible career."

"Well, you don't need to support me anymore." Darla raises her voice. "I'm moving out."

"Again? It's about time." Dad scowls.

"Charles!" Mom folds her arms.

"Stop it!" I yell. "All of you."

They all stare.

"For the record, I'm not going into theater because of Darla, and I'm not going into finance or business either. I'm not like any of you. And I can make it as a director. I know I can."

I snatch up my glasses before taking the stairs two at a time to my room.

* * *

The next day before first class. Shoes squeak on the scuffed floors. Lockers slam. Kids jostle in the hall. The smell of freshly baked muffins wafts from the cafeteria.

After helping Darla pack her rusty old car with boxes, I came to school early to meet with Joseph

Chan, a friend from stage crew who agreed to run the lights and sound for my play. I need to keep trying to make my play work, no matter what, and I didn't want to be at home for Darla's farewell with my parents. Now I'm hurrying toward my math class, with George at my heels.

Strangely, George remembered to come to the meeting, although his ideas were a little wild—maybe purple disco lights aren't required.

"I need you to write down all the lighting and sound cues we discussed." I hope that he can help me out if I give him specific tasks to do and check up on him. "And maybe you could print neatly? The stage manager calls the cues during the performances, so it would help if you can read them."

"Uh, sure." George nods. He's playing the good guy, like in French class when everyone behaves extra well after Madame Bouchard has screamed at a student.

"Thanks, George. See you at rehearsal tomorrow."

He nods as we part ways, just as Ratna catches up to me, her eyes wild.

"Briar! What's going on?" She grips my arm and squeezes. "Clayton's wrist is in a cast. Sonata and Mica aren't talking. My play is a mess!"

"I know." I take a deep breath, feeling horrible. "Just calm down. I'm going to work it out." I try to sound convincing.

"How can you?" Her voice rises. "Everyone's saying *Wish Upon a Star* is cursed. I can't have my first play ruined."

My face heats up. I glance around, holding my director's binder in front of me like a shield, trying not to imagine who's gossiping about me. "I'm not completely sure how to fix it yet, but I'm thinking about it. Anyway," I add, desperate to offer Ratna a glimmer of hope, "my aunt Darla says that rehearsals always fall apart two weeks before opening."

"Is this the same aunt who can't keep a job?" Her eyes are brimming with tears. "How is that comforting?"

I swallow hard. "It isn't, really. But freaking out isn't going to help either." I give her a quick hug. "I've got to get to math now, but I promise the play will be everything you wanted."

"Really?" Her dark eyes are pleading.

"Really." I cross my fingers, hoping I can keep this promise. "I won't let you down."

Ten

Whitlock cafeteria. The next day after school. Rehearsal (although it's more like torture in a medieval dungeon).

When I enter the room on Friday after school, the sideways glances begin. Lorna stares outright. Everyone's eyes seem like dagger points aimed at me.

There she is, I imagine someone saying, as if my entrance is an event worth watching—like a stoning.

I'd hate to be in her cast, another probably adds.

She's too inexperienced to direct, Lorna's sure to be whispering.

Their words are the clink of gears on a torture device, a rack slowly dislocating my bones.

Ratna's not much better. Her face tells me how uptight she is. I have to pull off a miracle for her and for my cast.

My actors are sitting at a table near our usual spot by the recycling and garbage bins. Clayton's right forearm is in a cast, and he's wearing a sling. Sonata and Mica are on either side of him, looking anywhere but at each other. My throat tightens—I feel sorry for them. They're probably hating this moment as much as I am.

Then Samuel sweeps past me on the way to his crew.

"Ignore the gossip." He leans in to whisper, his long hair brushing my shoulder. "Anyone who directs Sonata has a hard time. And Clayton's broken arm isn't your fault."

His words give me strength. I try to smile.

I collect George, who's chatting with one of Samuel's actors, and approach my cast. Empower them, I think. But I'm not sure how.

Then I notice Mr. Ty. He's set up near my corner with a stack of marking, obviously keeping an eye on me—the problem director.

No pressure.

My hands begin to sweat.

I nudge my glasses farther up my nose and slide onto the bench across from Clayton. George sits next to me. Mica is hunched over, and Sonata stares stonily into space. I open my mouth to deliver the speech I planned—about how we've had our share of troubles, but we can overcome them if we each play our parts. But even I don't believe it.

So I'm left staring at them for an awkward moment, until I decide to face the gossip head on.

"So, our play is cursed." I wipe my palms on my jeans. "At least, that's what I hear."

Mica studies me, his forehead knotted. Sonata scowls, her eyes flicking to Lorna. Clayton and George exchange a startled look.

"But I'm not willing to give up," I say. "So I want to hear from you. We have less than two weeks to get this thing right. How do you think we can do that?"

Sonata's eyes narrow. "You're asking for our ideas?" She sounds exhausted.

"I guess I am."

"That's a first." She leans back, taking in the six other rehearsals. "To start, we should practice somewhere else. This place is toxic."

"That's actually a good idea." George nods.

"Don't sound so surprised." Sonata glares.

"I like it too," I say quickly, before a fight erupts. "George, can you book the rest of our rehearsals in our performance room? If we can't get it, any classroom will do."

"Yeah, sure," George says eagerly.

"Thanks." I'll need to check later that he's done it.

Then Sonata starts in on all the blocking she doesn't like. I stiffen, trying to listen without interrupting her. Finally, I say, "I'll think about your ideas. We can try out some of them in rehearsal, but remember that I have the final say."

Sonata sucks in her cheeks and says nothing.

Mica is still withdrawn. I don't want to force him to speak, so I move on to Clayton.

"What about you, Clayton?" I ask.

"Huh?"

Inspiring Clayton may be impossible. "Well," I begin, "I know you haven't been comfortable with your character—the glitter and all. Since I have to work out costumes over the next week, I thought maybe we could tweak things, help you find a way into this character."

"I guess." Clayton gives the usual shrug, but he seems relieved. Maybe I should have listened to him earlier.

"What about his arm?" Sonata says. "Since when does a Star have a broken arm?"

"Maybe he's a fallen star?" George asks.

Mica snorts. Sonata raises one eyebrow.

"You know, that could actually work." I scribble a note to myself, thinking how we could add in a line or two, with Ratna's approval. "Okay, enough chatting." I stand up before Sonata can object to George's idea.

I grab my backpack off the floor, ready to reveal my new warm-up plan.

"I want to start today's rehearsal with a game of Twister." I pull the spinner and mat from my backpack.

Everyone looks surprised.

"Why?" Sonata's tone is cold.

"I knew you'd ask." I smile, even though I'm not sure if Twister will do what I want it to. "It'll remind us that this Fringe Festival is supposed to be fun. And"—I glance from Mica to Sonata—"it'll help us get more comfortable with one another."

"But it's a kids' game!" Mica says.

"Yup." I lay out the mat.

"How is Clayton supposed to do it?" Sonata's lip curls into a sneer.

"He can just use one arm. Let's get started. You too, George. I'll work the spinner." I give it a twirl. "Left foot on red," I announce.

People from other groups watch us curiously. I turn my back on them.

As we play, Mica avoids touching Sonata and ends up pretzeled at one end of the mat. Wiry Clayton is surprisingly good at it even with only one arm. George is having too much fun to care whether he wins. Sonata places each hand or foot precisely on the mat.

When George finally makes everyone collapse in a heap, Mica leaps up while the others laugh. From across the room, Samuel gives me a thumbs-up. A few actors watch as if they want to join in. Mr. Ty nods, which is great.

But I still need to get the play working.

We run through a few scenes. When I incorporate two of Sonata's blocking ideas, her shoulders relax slightly. And Sonata and Mica's stage chemistry isn't too horrible. Sonata is more aloof now, which works well with her character's failing marriage. Mica's hurt expression fits better since his character doesn't understand why his wife is so demanding. It must be hell for Mica to act with Sonata now that she's rejected him.

Eventually, we wrap up and head out. Mr. Ty follows me, his pile of marking under one arm.

"Twister was a nice touch," he says. "How did you come up with it?"

A grin spreads across my face. "I just grabbed it out of my closet this morning. I thought it might help." I don't tell him that I was staring hopelessly around my room, desperate to find some way to get Sonata and Mica to work together.

"Good instincts." Mr. Ty opens the cafeteria door for me.

"Thanks." I walk through feeling eight feet tall, until I see Mica scurrying down the hall like a wounded animal and Sonata striding the opposite way.

I shrink down to size.

Obviously, one good rehearsal is not enough.

Eleven

Outside Whitlock. Monday after school. A stream of students follows the worn path through the trees to the street. The smell of cigarettes wafts from the smokers' corner, near the sidewalk.

I trudge toward the bus stop. A squirrel leaps over some dandelions with more energy than I have. Today's rehearsal was exhausting, but at least we've blocked the whole play—finally.

I catch sight of Mica up ahead. His shoulders are rounded, and his head droops. God, he's taking Sonata's rejection hard. In rehearsal, Sonata was as high-strung as usual, and she looked right through Mica when they were offstage. Nice.

I hurry to catch up with him, thinking I can take him to Bean Me Up for a coffee and a pep talk—until I remember that's where it all went wrong for him.

I change my tactic.

"Hey, Mica?" I fall in step with him. "Do you like frozen yogurt? Now that the weather's warmer, I have this craving for pistachio yogurt at Menchie's, and...well...do you want to come?"

He nods. "I like that place."

"Great. Are you busy now?" I remember how he used to try to get Sonata to go for coffee with him after rehearsal.

"Uh, no." He kicks a stone along the path.

It's a five-minute walk in the opposite direction from Bean Me Up. We talk about his character on the way over—how oblivious Martin Wright is when Sylvia throws a slipper at him.

"He can be thick-skinned," Mica says.

"Nothing like you." I smile.

When we arrive, the shop is crowded with loud preteen girls who seem to fluster him. The bright décor is almost gaudy, and the girl behind the counter is overly cheerful.

We each grab a waffle bowl. I go for a nonfat pistachio yogurt with hot fudge, while Mica gets Red Velvet Royale with jelly beans, marshmallows and anything else he can pile on it. Then we escape to the patio overlooking the tree-lined side street.

Mica hunches over his bowl and digs in. I put my feet up on a nearby chair and take a bite of waffle mixed with yogurt, which tastes fabulous, as usual. I wonder how I can help Mica get over Sonata, or at least be able to tolerate her presence. Twister warm-ups are a start. Still, it's obvious that he's hurting.

"In the play, Sylvia's too hard on Martin." I keep my tone casual, even though I'm thinking about how Sonata's been too hard on Mica. "He's not perfect, but everyone deserves respect."

"Yeah." He takes a huge bite of yogurt.

"He doesn't talk about his feelings, but I think she really upsets him."

He looks sideways at me, still chewing. "It's a comedy, Briar."

"It has a serious side too." I twirl my spoon in my yogurt.

"I guess."

"Sylvia's giving up on a good guy," I say.

Mica swipes his hair out of his eyes. "Who are we talking about here? Sylvia or Sonata?"

"What do you mean?" I widen my eyes and pretend not to get it.

Mica shakes his head. "You're so subtle."

"I'm just saying that Martin has a lot to offer. Maybe he needs to find a different girl. One who suits him better." I stuff my mouth full of yogurt.

Mica stares into the distance. "Maybe you're right."

* * *

The main-floor drama room. Wednesday after school. One week to opening.

I arrive at rehearsal with a box of costumes and props. Sonata, Clayton and George are already there. Mica follows me in. When he tries to help carry my load, I brush him off.

"I've got a surprise!" My voice rises. I'm so much happier rehearsing away from Lorna and the others.

"I hope you're not putting me in an ape suit." Mica smirks.

"How'd you guess?" I say. After our frozen yogurt, he's more relaxed with me, although he still avoids Sonata when he can.

"I don't like surprises," Sonata says.

"It's not really for you." I won't let her ruin my good mood. "It's for Clayton."

"Me?" Clayton squirms.

"I promised I'd rework your character, and I did." I rifle through the clothes. "Can you moonwalk?"

"What? Why?"

"I've heard you're in hip-hop club, so I know you can move." I glance up at him. "But moonwalking?"

Clayton gives me a quizzical look. Then he jumps onto the stage and moonwalks across it.

George hoots. Even Sonata applauds.

I pick up his costume, piece by piece, and pass it to him. A black faux-leather suit with a pink shirt and bow tie, and a single white rhinestone glove—all from the Whitlock costume room. "Looks like you earned these."

"What's going on?" Sonata says. "Briar—"

"Let me explain." I hold up my hands. "The word 'star' has two meanings. Clayton's character is a star in the sky, but he can also be the other type of star." I pause as everyone stares at Clayton's costume. "I'm playing our Star character with a Michael Jackson theme."

"What?" Sonata gapes.

Mica nods at Clayton. "You even look a bit like him."

"Cool," George says.

A grin creeps across Clayton's face.

"Each time you're about to come onstage, we'll play the beginning of 'Billie Jean,' and then you can moonwalk in," I say. "Michael Jackson wore an outfit like this one in his music video, and he first did the moonwalk during a performance of 'Billie Jean.'"

"I suppose that will work, but what about his broken arm?" Sonata gestures at Clayton's cast and sling.

"Ratna's added two new lines. The first time we see the Star, Sonata will say, 'What happened to your arm?' And then Clayton will say, 'I fell.'"

George snorts. "It's my fallen star idea!"

"Yup. I hope it'll get a laugh." I turn to Clayton. "So what do you think? It'll modernize the play— we'll set it in the eighties instead of the fifties."

Clayton pulls on the glove. "I can get into this."

"Great!" I say, relieved.

"What will Mica and I wear?" Sonata eyes the rest of the pile I've lugged in.

"I'm sticking with mismatched outfits for Sylvia and Martin." I show everyone a plaid suit for Mica and a dress with a zigzag print and fluffy orange slippers for Sonata. I also have the multicolored apron that Darla gave to Mom and two of Mom's dishtowels. "I hope the clothes fit."

The jacket is too big for Mica, but it's better than too small. Sonata slips behind a curtain to change into the dress. It fits her beautifully— she looks good no matter what she wears. With his small frame, pert nose and curly black hair, Clayton pulls off a terrific Michael Jackson.

George takes photos of them for the program— my Martin, Sylvia and Star. They're so perfect, it makes my eyes water.

Mica, Sonata and Clayton change back into their regular clothes for rehearsal. George and I take our positions in the audience. The opening scene goes well, but Mica's acting is flat in the slipper-throwing sequence.

"Okay," I say. "Let's run through that scene again, but this time—"

"Not again, Briar!" Sonata's neck muscles are pulled tight. "We need to—"

"Thanks, but I'll decide what we rehearse." I ignore her dark look. "Although I do want to talk about your character's needs in this scene," I say, crossing my fingers that she'll cooperate. "What do you think Sylvia wants?"

Sonata leans against our makeshift sink, sighing loudly. "She wants to get Martin's attention, to make him notice her now that he's home. She doesn't want him to work after dinner, like he always does."

"Great. I love the detail about working after dinner." I praise her, since she really does know how to get into character. "And what are your character's objectives here, Mica?"

He glances at Clayton, who shrugs. "Uh, I'm not sure," he finally says.

Sonata folds her arms, frowning. "Martin wants to—"

"Let Mica do it," I interrupt. Spots of color appear on her cheeks. I turn to him. "Okay, Mica. Let me say it this way. What does your character want at this moment in the play?"

"Uh"—he examines the stage lights—"to understand?"

George gives him a thumbs-up.

"Good." I nod. "Can you get more specific? To understand what?"

"I'm not sure."

"Well, Martin asks Sylvia if she hired a chef. So what clue does that give? Does he want to understand why she threw a slipper at him?"

"No. He wants his dinner."

"Great. When does he want his dinner?"

"Now."

"Why?"

He fidgets. "Because he's hungry. He missed lunch because of a meeting."

"That's it! That's Martin's objective in this scene. Let's run through it again with that in mind."

"Okay." Mica wipes his sweaty forehead.

I smile as Mica delivers his lines perfectly, glancing around the kitchen in hopeful anticipation of a delicious meal.

We stay late to work through the rest of the play, pausing for side coaching when the action gets dull. Even Clayton manages to deliver his lines with more emotion than usual, and no one objects when I schedule an extra practice for the next night.

At the end of the rehearsal, Clayton sidles over.

"When I auditioned, I wanted an action part—like maybe a cop. But now..." He pauses. "Playing the Star is cool. Thanks."

"No problem. Now will you memorize all your lines?"

He moonwalks away from me. "You got it," he says.

Twelve

The main-floor drama room—again. Friday after school.

I practically live here these days, but it's worth it.

At our extra rehearsal last night, we worked on scene transitions and making eye contact with other actors. Clayton and Mica managed to stay in character, most of the time. And Sonata only tried to take over the rehearsal three times.

Today, my actors are finishing the last few lines of our first full run-through with props. No stopping for director notes. No stopping for Sonata to argue with my decisions. I stare intensely, imagining how the audience will react to each scene and figuring out what tweaks I still need to make.

It helps that I can also watch my first two audience members other than George and me. Ratna and Samuel lean forward in their seats—so far, they've laughed in the right places. I've promised to watch Samuel's show later, as his play will be staged here during Fringe Festival too.

Dust motes float in the beams of light. The stage creaks with Mica's footsteps. It's not a perfect performance of *Wish Upon a Star*, but the entrances and exits are working, Clayton has remembered most of his lines, his cast and sling work onstage, and Sonata and Mica are a believable married couple, complete with emotional baggage.

As my actors perform the curtain call I planned, Ratna leaps to her feet, clapping. Samuel grins at me before he whistles and claps too.

My first applause is sweet. I finally have hope that we can pull off a decent show, earning me a spot in Mr. Ty's directing workshop.

"Awesome work, everyone!" I say as George emerges from backstage, where he's been assisting with props and calling the cues. "We can still make some adjustments at the tech and dress rehearsals next week, but other than that we're good to go."

Mica and Clayton beam. George fist-pumps the air. Sonata hurries off the stage, rubbing her temples.

"It's incredible to see my words performed!" Ratna's eyes shine.

"You've done a great job." Samuel gives me a quick hug. Maybe it wouldn't be so bad to go out with him—after Fringe is over, of course.

"Thanks. I bet your play is great too," I say.

"You'll find out soon enough." Samuel hurries to the hall to collect his actors and props.

"You're an excellent Sylvia," Ratna says to Sonata.

Strangely, Sonata pushes past Ratna, ignoring the compliment. "I have a headache." She rushes toward the exit. Her eyes are fever-bright, her movements jerky.

"What about my director notes?" I straighten my glasses.

Sonata keeps walking, her back stiff. I frown— she's been a pain during most of our rehearsals, just the way Samuel said she would be.

"Remember, we'll be doing the tech rehearsal on Monday night, the dress rehearsal on Tuesday and then our performances Wednesday to Saturday," I call as she disappears. "Don't be late!"

And she's gone. I wonder for a moment what's got into her. But she always performs well—even when she's challenging me—so I let it go.

* * *

Madame Bouchard's French class. Monday morning. Fifteen minutes until lunch.

I spent the weekend planning and replanning my tech rehearsal, fussing over the details. Now I'm watching the clock from the back row of desks, too jittery to conjugate verbs, waiting to meet with Joseph and George at lunch to finalize the sound and lighting cues on paper.

I tap my pen against my desk and stare out into the empty hallway. My lighting is simple—the lights fade up at curtain rise, dim during the night scenes, go glittery when the Star appears and fade out at the end of the play. The set and props are in place—I have my original sink-and-counter set with a new eighties-style wooden table and chairs. The props are mostly kitchenware I found in the prop room and at thrift stores. For sound, I'm using an instrumental jazz version of "When You Wish Upon a Star" just before curtain rise, and "Billie Jean" each time the Star appears.

It's a weird thought, but my job is almost done, since the stage manager calls the cues during the shows. Soon I'll be watching the performances from the tech booth, hungry for the audience's applause and worrying about what might go wrong.

"Briar!" Madame Bouchard shouts. "*Avez-vous entendu l'annonce?*"

I jump and drop my pen. She's halfway up the aisle, staring me down. "*Pardon, Madame?*" I say with a lousy French accent. Most of the class has turned to watch the showdown.

Madame Bouchard gestures at the loudspeaker on the wall. "You have been called down to the guidance office." She speaks with a thick French accent. "Get your books and go. I will expect your conjugation work on my desk by next class."

Guidance? What the hell? I can't be late for my meeting.

"*Oui, Madame.*" I pick up my pen, grab my binders and take off.

The guidance office is on the other side of the school from the cafeteria, where Joseph and George expect to meet me. I'm calculating how long it will take to get there as I hurry into the office to find Principal Racier and Mr. Ty standing with Mica, Clayton, George and Ratna.

"What's going on?" I sidle up to Ratna.

"I have no idea." She fidgets with the sleeves of her sweater.

Principal Racier looks official in her black pin-striped jacket and skirt. Mr. Ty's face is more serious than I've ever seen it. My stomach goes fluttery. Is this about *Wish Upon a Star*? Did George do something crazy again? Where's Sonata?

Principal Racier clears her throat. "Sit down, everyone." She gestures at the seven chairs already arranged around a low table.

Mr. Ty shuts the door to the hall. Mrs. Maietta, one of the guidance counselors, emerges from her tiny office and leans against the doorframe.

We single-file around the table, trading questioning looks, and take our seats. Mr. Ty sits next to me. Principal Racier crosses her legs.

When she speaks, Principal Racier's voice is solemn. "I'm extremely sorry to tell you that Sonata is currently in the hospital and won't be returning to school for some time."

I'm floored. "What?"

Ratna goes pale. "She can't be."

"We know this is hard—" Mr. Ty begins.

"What's wrong with her?" Mica says.

"How are we gonna..." Clayton trails off as Principal Racier raises a hand to silence us.

"The family has given us permission to let you know that she had a breakdown due to stress," she says. "Her close friends know as well, although we're not spreading the news to the general population. So, please, no Facebook posts, no tweets."

"Oh my god." My voice cracks. Sonata was that close to the edge? How did I miss it?

"How could this happen to her?" George asks.

"Sonata's so good at everything." Ratna squeezes my hand.

"She's perfect." Mica has tears in his eyes.

The bell rings for lunch. Through the door, I can hear the hall filling with people. They'll be strolling to the cafeteria or rushing out to Bean Me Up like nothing has happened. I blink hard as my vision blurs.

"It's a lot to take in." Mr. Ty pats Mica on the shoulder.

Principal Racier's face is grim. "That's why Mrs. Maietta will be available to you if you need to talk."

"I'm here for you any time." Mrs. Maietta's tone is soothing.

"Is this because of the play?" I turn to Mr. Ty, my hand clutching Ratna's like it will keep me from drowning. Did I push Sonata too far? I should have known. I should have done something.

"It's no one's fault." Mr. Ty looks each one of us in the eyes. "But we do need to decide what to do about *Wish Upon a Star*."

A wave of despair washes over me. Sonata's been trouble since I cast her, but as long as she played her role without challenging me too much, I left her alone. What kind of heartless director am I? Why didn't I pay more attention?

The answer is horrifying: Because I was too focused on myself.

"We could withdraw your play from the festival or find a new actor who can learn the lines and blocking in two days," Mr. Ty continues. "It's a hard decision either way—one we don't want to make for you. Continuing the play may be what you need to do, or it may be too difficult."

Mica, Clayton, George and Ratna stare at me as if I should have the answer.

My heart thuds in my chest. I have no idea what to do.

Thirteen

An abandoned stage in a darkened drama room. Later that day. One lonely spotlight hits a sink. Another illuminates a wooden kitchen table and chairs.

Clayton slouches against the stage, ignoring his phone even though it's bleeping and blinking.

Mica paces the room, his fleshy arms clamped across his chest.

George lies on the floor in front of the stage, drumming on his leg with his fingers and staring up into the lighting grid.

Ratna shivers beside me, even though she's wearing a thick hoodie and tights.

I sit front row center in a stackable chair, digging my fingernails into my palms. I'm a director without a female lead. Or maybe I'm not a director at all.

Principal Racier excused us from afternoon classes, and somehow we all ended up at our set, bathed in semidarkness. We've each talked with Mrs. Maietta, one by one, and endured the stares and whispers in the hallways. Mrs. Maietta's speech felt rehearsed by the time I spoke with her. "A mental breakdown can occur when a person feels overwhelmed, highly anxious or depressed," she had said, adjusting her bra strap inside her floral dress. "It can be traumatic for everyone involved."

No kidding.

My brain and body are cycling through emotions so quickly, I can't keep up. I'm selfishly wishing this hadn't happened right before opening, and I'm horrified that it happened at all. The show must go on, they say, but even when Sonata is in the hospital?

"Maybe Ratna could play Sonata's part?" George drums faster.

I gaze at Ratna. I can't picture her as Sylvia no matter how hard I try.

"I wrote the lines, but I don't have them all memorized." Ratna rubs her arms as if she's cold. "Besides, I'm already in a play."

"But it's such a small role. You're only the bank teller." As George sits up, his face falls into shadow and his ears glow pink, lit from behind.

"Small roles matter too." Ratna frowns. "And Lorna would still have to fill it."

"Do you think Lorna knows?" Mica's eyes are hollow pits.

I wish I could comfort him somehow, but I can't even calm myself.

"Lorna wasn't in school today. And she rescheduled her tech rehearsal for tomorrow. She knows." Ratna nods.

Lorna was right about my play being cursed, I think.

"Everyone knows. There are a hundred posts on Sonata's Facebook page." Clayton takes off his sling and scratches the skin around his cast.

"What do they say?" George asks.

"Mostly 'get better soon' and 'we miss you.' That kind of stuff," Clayton says.

"Why do you think this happened?" George bangs his feet against the side of the stage.

"I heard she was in the psych ward last summer," Clayton begins.

"What?" I gape at him. Why didn't I know this?

"I don't want to talk about this." Mica's voice has a tremor in it.

"Yeah. Sorry." Clayton picks up his phone and fiddles with it, looking awkward. "It's just a rumor, anyway."

"Which hospital is she at?" I ask.

"East General. At least, that's what I heard." Clayton glances up. "Why? Are you going to visit her?"

"I should probably—"

"Can we just decide what to do about the play?" Mica stops in front of me, his face haggard, his bulky shape blocking my view of Clayton.

"Maybe Briar could play Sylvia," Ratna suggests. "She knows the lines and the blocking."

My stomach twists. "I'm a director, not an actor." I can't turn my director frames on myself. "Besides, it's Sonata's role." I sink further into guilt. Did I play a part in Sonata's breakdown?

"We can't find someone else in such a short time," George says.

"That's why we should withdraw from the festival." The words are out before I can stop them.

"What?" Ratna jumps up. "But Briar—"

"Sonata would want us to withdraw." Mica's lip trembles.

Clayton snorts. "How would you know? No one gets what's going on with Sonata or we would have seen this coming."

Mica looks offended, but I have to agree with Clayton.

"I say we do the show with Briar as Sylvia," George says.

"That's two of us!" Ratna's face brightens, but her eyebrows are still bunched. "Wouldn't Sonata want the show to go on? She put a ton of work into it."

"Without her?" Mica shakes his head.

They argue the options, over and over. I stare down at my hands, gripping the sides of the chair. Finally I say, "Shows do get cancelled sometimes. Maybe it's best."

"Exactly," Mica says.

"Just sleep on it, Briar," Ratna begs. "You could play Sylvia, if you—"

"Ratna, it's late. Let's go home." I stand and pick up my backpack. "George, can you cut the lights?"

Ratna sighs. George looks like he's going to speak, and then he walks to the lighting board at the back of the room.

I take off my glasses and stuff them into my pocket. It's over. My first directing job.

The stage lights fade to black.

*   *   *

Outside Briar's bungalow. Early evening. The front door is halfway open. Loud voices can be heard coming from inside the house.

I want to retreat to my bed. Curl up and pull the blankets over my head. But Darla and Mom are blocking the front hall, shouting.

"How could you lose another job?" Mom's face is red, and her freshly dyed hair is a mess. "When are you going to grow up?"

"It's not my fault!" Darla's beaded hair swings back and forth as she waves her arms. "The management at Finders Keepers is prehistoric."

Neither has noticed me. I hesitate on the front step. Do they have to fight today?

"What did you do, Darla?" Spit flies from Mom's lips. "Come in late too many times? Leave for lunch and skip the rest of the afternoon?"

"I come to my only sister when I need help, and this is what you say? I'm only asking to move back in for a couple of weeks."

"It's never just a couple of weeks!"

I step inside. "Mom! Darla!" I had planned to yell—make them shut up for once—but my voice comes out in a whimper.

They both turn to me.

My legs begin to shake. I grab onto the coat stand to steady myself.

"What's wrong?" Darla takes my backpack.

"Sonata..." I can barely whisper. "One of my actors...is in the hospital. She had a breakdown."

"Oh, baby." Mom pulls me against her, and I feel my tears well up. "How can we help?"

Darla rubs my back. My throat clogs. I have no words.

Fourteen

The hospital gift shop. Tuesday morning. A florist's fridge filled with bouquets of sweet-scented flowers. A rack of cheerful greeting cards. Shelves of cheap candies and plush toys.

The shop is deserted, except for a twenty-something woman behind the counter, flipping through a magazine and looking bored.

Mom and Dad dropped me off fifteen minutes ago, and I've circled the small shop twice, searching for some token to bring Sonata. As I stare at the shelves of stuffed rabbits, bears and monkeys, I can't fathom which one Sonata might like. As a director, you're supposed to understand every character in your play. It's harder still to understand your actors.

What pushed Sonata over the edge? Did she suffer some sort of trauma? Was she really in the psych ward last summer? What exactly is a breakdown, anyway? I have a million questions, and no right to ask them. But I'm going to see her anyhow.

I'm more than a little nervous about visiting the fourth floor—the psych ward—even though I phoned Sonata's mother last night to ask if it was okay to visit, and she told me what to expect. Calling Sonata's place was Mom's idea. Dad gave me money to buy Sonata a gift. Darla taught me a Reiki healing treatment to use on her, as if I'd really attempt it. At least Darla and my parents have stopped fighting for now, but with Darla moving back in, it won't last long.

I pick up a plush hedgehog that catches my eye. A white underbelly, soft fur on its back and adorable oversized eyes. *Comfort Creature*, the tag reads. *An emotional support animal with healing warmth and aromatherapy.* Apparently you can heat the hedgehog in the microwave and insert a pouch of lavender in its back.

I check out a few other animals, but when I find myself cuddling the hedgehog, I figure it'll do. Maybe I need an emotional support animal too.

I buy it and head to an elevator before I can change my mind about visiting. Today, I feel bruised. I've hardly slept. Every muscle aches. I'd rather be anywhere else.

I step into the elevator, hugging the hedgehog on the ride up.

I'm surprised that the fourth floor looks so ordinary—a nurses' station, wide hallways, open doors into patients' rooms. The lighting is fluorescent—glaring and too white. I consider how I'd light it for the stage, and then remember my glasses are at home. It's not like I need them anymore.

"May I help you?" A nurse with red hair and a purple uniform greets me.

"I'm...uh..." I fight an urge to flee—maybe this is a mistake. "I'm here to see Sonata Lopez."

"Sonata?" She tilts her head. "Oh, you mean Sarah. You must be Briar. Sarah's mother told us you'd be coming."

"Uh, yeah." I drop my backpack beside the desk. "I know I can't take this in, but is the hedgehog okay?"

She smiles. "Yes, although the hospital has a scent-free policy, so Sarah won't be able to use the aromatherapy until she goes home."

My face gets hot—I should have thought of that. Why do they even sell them in the gift shop?

"Please keep your visit to fifteen minutes." She has me sign the visitors' log. "Sarah's in room four twelve. I'll show you the way." She takes off down the hall, rubber shoes squeaking.

I resist peering into the open rooms as we pass, partly because I'm afraid of what I might see. When I do catch a glimpse of a patient in a doorway, it's a middle-aged man with bed head and a cheerless expression. I can't help wondering why he's here.

My pulse quickens as I near room four twelve. I don't know what to expect, even though her mother said that Sonata would want to see me, that she was upset about abandoning our play.

"Sarah, your visitor's here." The nurse raps on the open door before turning on her heel and heading back the way we came.

I hesitate—last chance to run for it—before entering the room, expecting to hear Sonata scolding the nurse for calling her Sarah.

But Sonata is hardly herself. Her face is gray, her hair is stringy, and she's wearing a ratty T-shirt and sweatpants. She sits in a chair near the window, with a box of tissues on her lap.

"Where are your glasses?" she asks.

"I'm...uh...not here as director." I squeeze the hedgehog.

"Oh." She stares blankly at me, as if it takes effort to concentrate or even care.

It's profoundly disturbing—the Sonata I know has vanished.

"I brought you this." I hold out the hedgehog, which seems ridiculous now.

"Thanks." Sonata takes it, gazes at it for a moment and then drops it in her lap.

On a nearby table there are several plants and a bouquet of yellow carnations with a florist card signed by Lorna. Sonata's bed is unmade, and the second bed isn't occupied. A stack of books sits on Sonata's side table. There's no TV in the room.

I clear my throat, aware of the murmur of people talking in the room across the hall. Sonata's room smells like antiseptic and questionable food from her leftover breakfast tray.

"How's the food?" I say, not sure how to start.

Sonata just shrugs. "I've eaten better."

I try to remember what I wanted to say, but it's abandoned me.

Sonata's hair falls across her face as her fingers creep up to probe her temples.

I try again. "I'm sorry this happened to you."

"I'm sorry I ruined the play." Tears well in Sonata's eyes and trickle down her cheeks.

I suck in a breath, horrified. I made her cry. Now what do I do?

"It's not your fault." I stumble over my words. "I should have noticed what was happening. I should have helped—"

"This has nothing to do with you, Briar." Her voice wavers.

"It doesn't?"

"No. I..." She takes in a deep breath as the tears well up again. "It's been building for a while. The pressure to do well in my courses, the commercials I've been shooting, the performances at school, the university auditions and applications. When I got a letter on Friday saying that I didn't get into the National Theatre School, I just... wanted to stop trying."

"Sonata, you didn't..." I shiver, unable to finish my thought. I have no right to ask.

She stares down at her hands. "No, but I had a bottle of pills." Her voice is hollow.

My own hands tremble. "Oh, Sonata! I'm so sorry." I'm not sure what else to say. Anything I can think of seems horribly inadequate.

The nurse pops her head in the room, nods and smiles at Sonata, then pops out again just as quickly.

Sonata grimaces. "They check me every fifteen minutes, even when I'm trying to sleep."

"I guess that's good. They're watching out for you."

"Yeah." Sonata rips a tissue out of the box and wipes her face. "How's everyone else? Are they mad?"

"No, they're upset. They miss you. We all do. The play is—"

"Canceled? Because of me?"

I nod. "Unless you think you'll be better..." I let the thought dangle, unfinished. It's a stupid idea.

She sighs and crumples the tissue in her fist, looking like she might cry again. "I'm so sorry, Briar. I hate that the play is canceled because of me. But please understand, I can't think about school or anything else right now. It's overwhelming. Even getting out of bed is a big step. I don't know how

I'm ever going to get back to Whitlock. I wish the play could go on, but not with me in it."

"That's fine," I choke out.

We talk for a few more minutes before she has to leave for her first group therapy session. As I watch her shuffle down the hall, a shell of herself, I feel completely powerless. If only I could remind her of what's fun about life, the theater, everything.

An uncomfortable thought nags at me. I could show her that life goes on, that the show goes on even if it seems impossible. Even if I have to perform onstage.

If anyone can save this play, it's me. After all, I've been breathing Sonata's lines for weeks, and the blocking is imprinted on my brain.

I text my cast, Ratna and George. Meet me on the set at noon. We have planning to do.

Then I phone Lorna.

Fifteen

On the set. Same day at lunchtime.

"We need to perform *Wish Upon a Star* for Sonata." I pace the stage, letting the spotlights shine down on me, squinting at Ratna, Mica, Clayton and George in the front row of seats. "I've been to see her, and she's upset about the play getting canceled. This is how we can help her—by performing the play for her, continuing on no matter how tough things get."

"Sonata wants this?" Mica peers up at me.

"Yup—she said she wishes the play could go on, and I want us all to do that for her. Joseph has agreed to record our first performance so we can show Sonata what we did. I want it to be a message from all of us—a way to encourage her to get better."

I don't mention that she was suicidal. Lorna knew, when I phoned her, but I doubt anyone else knows.

Mica nods thoughtfully.

"And you're going to play Sylvia?" Ratna's hand flies to her chest.

"I'm going to try." I bite my lip, hoping I can overcome my jitters to do a decent job. It's one thing to perform skits in drama class. It's another to act in front of a packed house.

"If you're acting, who's going to direct?" Clayton gestures with his cast.

"Briar can do both." George jumps onto the stage beside me. "Plenty of Hollywood directors star in their own films—"

"Sorry, George, but I can't see how the play is working when I'm onstage." I reach up to adjust my glasses, then realize they're still at home. "I'm going to need help with the directing. Sort of a co-director, although we'll still be using my vision for the play," I say a little forcefully.

"But who—" George begins just as Lorna walks in.

"Sorry I'm late." Lorna dumps her bag on a chair. "I had to get out of my afternoon classes."

George grins. Mica and Clayton exchange startled looks.

Ratna claps her hands. "Briar, you're brilliant."

* * *

Backstage on opening night. Three minutes to curtain rise. A jazzy version of the song "When You Wish Upon a Star" can be heard. Beyond the curtains, the buzz of the audience grows louder.

There's a sheen of sweat on Mica's forehead. Clayton adjusts his pink bow tie for the hundredth time and fiddles with his sling. The air is electrified. My skin tingles.

I fight the urge to go to the washroom yet again, and I fuss with the loose stitches where I took in Sylvia's zigzag-print dress and hemmed the bottom. I'm thinner and shorter than Sonata, with fewer curves in the right places, but enough of a contrast to work well with oversized Mica.

After a day and a half of frantic rehearsals, I'm terrified that I'll embarrass myself. I doubt I'll forget my lines, but the thought of all those eyes on me—probing me, evaluating me—turns my legs to jelly.

It's only a one-act play, I remind myself. Twenty minutes at the most. You can survive that long. I hope.

I had to let Lorna direct me. Tolerate the subtle changes she made to the blocking. Bite my tongue and work with her. And she knew what she was doing. Even I had to admit that.

Now I have to trust that George will do his job during the play, trust that the lights and sound will come together, trust that Clayton will remember his lines and Mica will show the character's emotions rather than his own.

"God, I can't take this," I whisper. "How does anyone do this?"

Mica squeezes my hand. Clayton does a quick moonwalk to entertain me—until he bumps into a prop box with a loud thud.

"Shhh." I smile, and then we're all giggling like kids at a sleepover.

"We'll be awesome," Clayton says.

"For Sonata." Mica's face goes serious.

I nod, jittery again. I peer out through a crack in the curtain to distract myself.

Samuel is in the front row, along with most of his cast. Aunt Darla is chatting loudly with a timid kid from grade nine. My parents are in the second-last row near the door—maybe they want a quick escape afterward. The rest of the audience is mostly students and teachers who have Whitlock Fringe Festival passes. Samuel's play will run shortly after mine, and two other plays are happening now in other drama rooms. Fringe is a terrific event, and most of the school comes out to it. Too bad I'm too nervous to enjoy it.

I think about how the audience is reading our revised program, which now lists Lorna as co-director and me in the role of Sylvia. They're reading our co-directors' statement, which explains my vision for the play and includes these words: *This performance is dedicated to Sonata Lopez.* I got teary when I wrote it.

Lorna and Ratna are at the back of the theater, smiling and talking. George is with Joseph in the tech booth behind them. George's hands flap

KAREN KROSSING

at his sides as if he can't keep them still. He's wearing a headset to call the cues.

The house lights fade out. The music too. The stage grows dark.

In the weak lights backstage, I shoot a desperate look at Mica, who looks as nervous as I feel, and plunge into the semidarkness onstage, taking my first position. Sylvia's sink is now aimed slightly toward the audience so that they can see my face.

The curtains swing back. The stage lights fade up.

A sudden panic wells inside me. I can't do this! What was I thinking? I want my director frames back. I can't face an audience without them.

Then I hear Lorna's voice in my head. *Look just above their heads when you gaze at the stars.* That one direction grounds me.

I stand before a sink full of dirty dishes, staring out the window. It's late evening. Martin, my husband, sits alone at the kitchen table, eating.

"'The stars are out tonight,'" I begin.

Martin gnaws at his burnt steak.

Sixteen

Halfway through the play. Lights heat up the stage. The audience is cloaked in blackness.

The Star waits in the wings for his first cue. Martin sleeps in a kitchen chair, his feet up and his neck at an awkward angle. The remains of a midnight snack lie scattered across the table in front of him.

Find your light, Lorna had said. I step down-stage into a spotlight pool, grateful that the beam masks the audience, even though I can still hear them breathing, rustling programs, muffling coughs.

"'Star light, star bright...'" I begin Sylvia's wish, but I'm wishing too. Wishing that this play will make a difference to Sonata, wishing that I will survive four performances as Sylvia, wishing that I will return to directing as soon as possible, maybe in Mr. Ty's workshop. "'I wish I may, I wish I might, have the husband I wish tonight.'"

I squeeze my eyes shut, truly hoping that wishes can come true. I hold position for two beats before opening my eyes and looking dejectedly at Martin, whose snores make the audience laugh. I let my shoulders fall.

"'I should have known.'" I project my voice to the back of the room, keeping a gloomy tone.

Then "Billie Jean" begins to play, and the glittery light effect comes on. I look startled, spinning to watch as the Star moonwalks to center stage.

A roar of laughter greets the Star, who grins.

I'm thrilled at the response, but I tuck the feeling away for later. "'You're...you're glowing!'" I say to the Star as the music fades. "'Who are you?'"

"'I'm a Star.'" He does a little dance move, emphasizing his cast and sling. The audience laughs again.

"'What happened to your arm?'"

"'I fell.'" The Star shrugs.

More laughter.

"'You heard my wish?'" I clasp my hands.

"'We all did.'" The Star gestures at the sky outside. "'But it was a little vague. I need a clear directive, you know? What do you want to...uh... change about your husband?'"

"'Everything!'" I throw a disgusted look at Martin. "'I wish for you to make him more attentive—he works too much. And can you make him funnier?'"

Martin lets out another snore, on cue.

"'And the snoring? Can you get rid of that? Also, he talks with his mouth full—I hate that...'" My list gets longer.

The Star steps back. I pursue him, still talking.

"'Whoa!'" he says. "'One wish per night— that's the deal.'"

"'That's hardly enough.'" I frown, pretending to ponder my options. "'Okay. I wish he was romantic! He's never—'"

"'Are you sure that's what you want?'" The Star taps one toe impatiently.

"'Why wouldn't it be?'"

The Star does a funky dance move, and the glittery light effect gets stronger.

"'Done!'" he announces. Then he vanishes.

Martin wakes as if on command, sees me and begins walking seductively toward me. It's hilarious, at least to the audience. It makes me a little uncomfortable, but I'm doing this for Sonata.

Martin serenades me by crooning old Elvis songs, and he tries to eat strawberries off my toes. After he composes bad poetry for me, I've had enough. Once Martin finally falls asleep, I'm at the window begging for the Star to undo the wish.

The Star appears with the usual glitter and music. "'You again?'" He frowns. "'Don't you know that you get one wish a night? I need some cloud cover to get away from you!'"

"'But I just want you to undo my old wish,'" I plead.

"'Why should I?'"

"'Because it wasn't really what I wanted.'" I begin to sob—it took me a while to learn to cry on demand. Lorna suggested I mine my life for something sad. Picturing Sonata with a bottle of pills makes me teary every time. "'Can I just have my husband back?'" I say to the Star. "'This one is too...excitable.'"

The audience laughs on cue.

"'This happens all the time.'" The Star rolls his eyes. "'You humans wish for what you want, but it's rarely what you need.'"

I think about Sonata, who needs the support of her friends.

Martin croons an Elvis song in his sleep.

I cringe. "'Please, please, take back my wish,'" I beg the Star.

"'Fine.'" He scowls.

The stage flashes with glittery lights. When it's over, the Star has disappeared.

Martin wakes with a start. "'Sylvia, I've had the strangest dream! There were strawberries and...'" He blinks at the half-empty bowl of berries. "'What happened?'"

"'Everything's okay now, Martin.'" I kiss his cheek. "'I have what I need.'"

Martin's eyes find mine. He grips both my hands. "'So do I.'"

There's a long moment in which we embrace. The audience is dead quiet. Did we lose them?

The lights fade out. There's a lengthy beat of silence. Then the applause is deafening.

The curtains close. I squeal and dive at Mica and Clayton in the semidarkness, barely missing

Clayton's cast as we hug one another, even though we're a sweaty mess from the heat of the lights.

"I can't wait until tomorrow night." Mica beams.

"You can direct me any time." Clayton fist-bumps me.

"But Lorna—"

"This was your baby," Clayton says. "Don't kid yourself."

Then we're all laughing. We pull it together long enough to do the curtain call.

Samuel starts the standing ovation and everyone follows, even my parents. We bow again and again until the applause finally ends.

I'm still flying high when Ratna hugs me. "You did it! You did it! You did it! Thanks for making my play so awesome! How could I ever doubt you?"

Samuel pats me on the back, grinning, and then takes off to prepare his cast. Darla kisses both my cheeks, raving about the magic of live theater.

"You were great, Briar," Lorna says when she finds me.

"With a little help from my excellent co-director," I say.

I'm pushing my way toward the tech booth—I have a recording to pick up from Joseph—when my parents stop me.

"Directing and acting—you've been busy." Dad's smile reaches his eyes.

"That's my last acting gig," I say. "I'll be directing the next one."

"I'm sure you'll do a great job." He nods.

"We can't wait to see it," Mom adds.

I don't know if that means there'll be fewer arguments about my directing, but at least they appreciated this show. Baby steps, I think.

Then I head to the tech booth to find Joseph.

* * *

Sonata's hospital room. Late afternoon. The day after Fringe Festival. More flowers decorate her window ledge, soaking up the sun.

Sonata and I are squished onto her hospital bed, its head raised, with my laptop across our legs.

We're watching a performance of *Wish Upon a Star*, each with one earbud from my headphones to hear the dialogue. I got special permission from the nurses for the viewing.

"I can't believe you pulled this together in under two days!" Sonata says after the curtain call. She's lost weight, but her hair is washed and pulled up in a messy ballet bun. It's a huge improvement.

"Yeah, we needed more time." My director glasses slide down my nose, and I cringe to think of my own performance, although Mica and Clayton were pretty good.

"You did fine, Briar." She puts a hand on mine. "Thanks."

"For what?" I pretend to be oblivious.

"For keeping the play going when I couldn't. You even worked with Lorna, which isn't easy."

"She's not so bad." I smile. "Although next time I'd cast differently for Sylvia. Maybe someone taller, more graceful, with long dark hair and a stronger stage presence?" I stare intently at her.

"Maybe you'll find someone like that next year." Her eyes dart away.

"I doubt it. She'll probably be gone to university somewhere."

"Maybe not." Her hands skate over one another. "I may lose my grade-twelve year, and I don't know what's happening with university, so..."

"Whatever happens, at least you're thinking about the future." Just like Darla, who's moving to California with a friend she met at Finders Keepers. Apparently, they're both disillusioned by the "corporate agenda," so they're going to the land of sun to set up a vegan hotdog cart, with a little starter money from my surprisingly supportive parents. "You're a brilliant actor, Sonata," I say.

"Well, I'm good at acting happy, but that only works for so long."

"Mr. Ty thinks you're a brilliant actor too. He admitted you into the exclusive acting workshop."

"He did? Even though I'm not in school?"

"I guess he's hoping you'll come back. We all are."

She shudders. "First I need to get out of here— go home. One step at a time." She pauses. "Who got into the directing workshop?"

I grin. "Lorna, Samuel and me, as well as one other guy from grade eleven. I can't wait to start." Even if I have to work with Lorna again.

"Congrats. You've worked hard for it." Sonata gives me a sincere smile.

"No kidding." I pull out a copy of the playbill for *Wish Upon a Star* and hand it to her. "I also have this for you."

She opens it to the dedication. "Oh, Briar." Her eyes get misty.

"Check the back." I flip it over. "It's signed by all of us, as well as Lorna, Samuel, Mr. Ty and some other Fringe people."

"Wow!" Sonata reads the notes scribbled in the margins and over the advertisement for the end-of-year musical—I wouldn't mind directing that. "How were the other Fringe performances?"

"Would you like to see for yourself?"

"What? You mean—"

"I have them all here." I open a new folder on my computer. "Which one first? How about Please, Mr. Bank Manager, Save My Mother?"

Sonata adjusts her earbud. "Perfect." Her face brightens.

Empower your actors, Mr. Ty had suggested. I'm just grateful it works offstage as well.

We lean back against the hospital bed, knees up. The sun beams through the window like a spotlight, warming the room.

I click *Play*.

Acknowledgments

This book is possible because my daughters, Paige and Tess, shared stories about their arts high school—Rosedale Heights School for the Arts in Toronto. Thanks for letting me absorb the atmosphere of this dynamic school so that I could create this story. Thanks also to my early readers, who offered astute feedback: Pat Bourke, Paige Krossing, Tess Krossing, Patricia McCowan, Karen Rankin, Rilla Ross and Erin Thomas. My respect and admiration go to Sarah Harvey, editor at Orca Book Publishers, for creating the Limelights series and providing her usual wit, diligence and care in editing the manuscript. I'm grateful to the entire talented Orca team for helping to produce this book. Last but never least, thanks to my partner, Kevin, for his unfailing support.

KAREN KROSSING is addicted to stories. She studied English and drama at university before she began to write novels and short stories for children and teens. Karen also encourages new writers through workshops for kids, teens and adults. She lives with her family in Toronto, Ontario. *Cut the Lights* is her fifth novel. For more information, please visit karenkrossing.com.

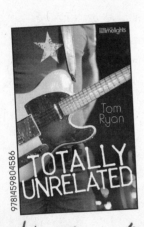